"True to its title, *Anomia* resists c … the divides between genres, gend… finely tuned prose, **Jade Wallace** moves with humanity and grace between the three worlds of a compellingly original cast of characters as they grapple with the complexities of love and loss, the necessity of sacrifice, and the magnitude of the unknown. A novel unlike anything you've read before."

— **Corinna Chong**
author of *Bad Land* and *The Whole Animal*

"A town out of time, a found community whose softness endures in the face of an uncaring society, and an ethereal and multifaceted love story disguised as mystery, *Anomia* is a haunting narrative of loss and longing. With mycelial plotting propelled by **Jade Wallace**'s nuanced and atmospheric prose, *Anomia* is an astonishing debut."

— **Michael Melgaard**
author of *Not That Kind of Place* and *Pallbearing*

"The unseen, the secret, the mystery. Against the rural backdrop of **Jade Wallace**'s *Anomia*, these three elements entangle in an intergenerational and interspecies story of paranoia and intimacies. In the face of the ongoing and often uncaring world of natural decay and animal life, the privacies and pain of each character are both enormous and minuscule in scale. *Anomia* is the sum of its many multiple parts, a whirling, delightful strange weaving of friendships, suspicion, and small town conspiracy."

— **Aaron Tucker**
author of *Soldiers, Hunters, Not Cowboys* and *Catalogue d'oiseaux*

ANOMIA

JADE WALLACE

ANOMIA

Published by Palimpsest Press

Printed and bound in Canada

Cover design and book typography by Obscure Design

Edited by Aimée Dunn

Copyedited by Mark Laliberte

Palimpsest Press would like to thank the Canada Council for the Arts and the Ontario Arts Council for their support of our publishing program. We also acknowledge the assistance of the Government of Ontario through the Ontario Book Publishing Tax Credit.

LIBRARY AND ARCHIVES CANADA CATALOGUING IN PUBLICATION

TITLE: Anomia / Jade Wallace.
NAMES: Wallace, Jade, author.
IDENTIFIERS: Canadiana (print) 20240366565
　　　　　　　Canadiana (ebook) 20240366573

ISBN 9781990293757 (softcover)
ISBN 9781990293764 (EPUB)

SUBJECTS: LCGFT: Detective and mystery fiction.
　　　　　LCGFT: Gothic fiction.
　　　　　LCGFT: Novels.

CLASSIFICATION: LCC PS8645.A467368 A83 2024 | DDC C813/.6—dc23

"There's not a name for every thing."

— **Harry Dodge**

THEY

There are times when all gestures feel like reenactments, when life and death are clouds that cannot be pulled apart, and it is then that Slip goes to the Unwood. The underbrush murmurs, giving away the rats as they crawl into hiding on their small paws. Birds vanish with a clapping of wings. Stones are rough-skinned and heavy in the hand. Holding them, it is impossible to think that reality is an optical illusion, an aural delusion, or a trick of memory. Branches snap underfoot and human nerves crackle with the electricity of living things.

The Unwood is on the edge of Euphoria, the town where Slip was born and still resides, alongside some 40,000 others, a population that has changed little throughout the past several decades. If one takes the main street north out of the downtown, past the suburbs, through orchards and meadowland, just beyond the trailer park, to the forest, then, if willing, one can continue on foot through the thick and pathless plant growth. The venture seems senseless for a long while, which is probably why Slip has never met another human being there. That, of course, and the local lore, which has rendered the place perilous and macabre. With patience and skepticism, however, one can reach the Unwood, which is the name that the locals have given to the large clearing in the trees where everything that is other than a tree grows ardent and reckless.

It is not a trip to be made too often, especially for Slip, who is a little ghost of a person, diminutive in size as well as persona. Pigment has slithered from Slip's hair, soft tissue has fled from Slip's frame. A lifetime has sucked the calcium from Slip's skeleton. Even Slip's owl-round glasses are translucent, as though they too are disappearing. Yet those same long years of living have made the weekly trek into the Unwood necessary. Without children, without a living spouse, siblings, or parents, and with most acquaintances long since dead or their names forgotten, nearly everyone Slip meets these days is a stranger. And all strangers offer is irritation. Only the deer of the Unwood, wary at a distance and terrified up close, have retained their regard for Slip, who returns their favour.

Today, bending to press fingers to an aching right ankle, Slip glimpses spots of lightness among the grasses whose blades are wide as rope. The lightnesses, wax-white as Slip's hair, appear at first to be mushrooms, livid and smooth, gathered close in a fairy ring. Slip moves closer, crouches down gingerly, and brushes off the green. The mushrooms are bones. Whose bones? There is no taxonomist, no taxidermist, available to consult in the Unwood where humankind can be neither seen nor heard.

For all we know, the bones might have been scattered during a carnival of predators. A raucous and callow ritual, with vines hung for ratty streamers overhead, half-chewed meat strewn on the floor. After the party, only the detrivores would have remained to lick the plates.

Slip laboriously clears the flora from the bones, which form no discernible shape. The temptation to rationalize the bones into a skeleton is overwhelming. Once they are ordered, the bones might convey a different meaning. If Slip does nothing, the bones will soon be completely interred by verdure, which would not be so bad for the bones, but it would be a disappointing outcome for Slip. There is some worth in figuring out what kind of animal the bones used to be. Isn't there?

Stirring the bones from their rest profanes a sacred stillness. Nevertheless, Slip continues with the work: ruffling the feathers of ferns to see whether they conceal the last organs of a corpse, brushing soil away from its own protrusions, gathering the findings in an elegant mass. There are more bones than Slip expected, but also fewer, for though the bones are many there is no skull. Without the skull, it is hard for a layperson to make sense of the long, the short, the irregular, and the sesamoid bones, and even the other flat bones. Slip could as easily be looking at a horse as at a human being. Perhaps, if the ribs still formed a single cage, Slip could articulate the skeleton and get some sense of scale. Scattered as they are, the bones signify nothing but death.

As the light leaves the sky, Slip departs.

On the morning after finding the bones, Slip wakes early. Through the translucent muslin curtains of the trailer, the sky streams in like weak lavender tea that Slip swallows along with two white pills for the pains of a long yesterday, before returning to the Unwood.

Even sturdily stacked, as they have been since last night, the bones remain such a scant semblance of order amidst the chaos of wild that they are difficult to find a second time. Once they have been located again, Slip drapes a red wool scarf over them to mark their place. The scarf has been around as long as Slip can remember. As a child, it haunted the family home, a loyal spirit appearing across seasons, sometimes thrown over the arm of the rocking chair, sometimes balled up with the winter quilts. No one could recall to whom it originally belonged. When the last of Slip's parents died, years after Slip had moved in to care for them both, the ancestral heirlooms they left behind were all solid, practical items like cast iron skillets and thick wool scarves. Slip's two siblings, one long since estranged from the family, one too busy and successful to pay much attention when their parents were ailing, had been cut out of the will, a largely symbolic gesture since the siblings were unlikely in any case to have been interested in the low-value leftovers of their parents' life. It was Slip alone who extracted the relics and sold the home for a meagre profit, which was used to buy Slip's current trailer. After experimenting with existence in a spontaneous succession of provinces and territories, Slip returned resignedly to Euphoria, the very town where the journey began, which was, as it turned out, hardly worse than anywhere else.

With the old scarf as a guidepost to mark the pile of bones, Slip begins to spiral systematically outward, combing through grass for the missing skull, yearning to find it. The creature from whom the skeleton came must be a substantial one, for there are many bones. But without the head, the body is a useless globe stand.

Slip is disappointed several times by clustered mushrooms, large flakes of white birch bark, pale stones. Overhead, the robins and warblers are all jaw in the dawn air, as though they too are searching for something. Pawing through the greenery begins to feel like hunting or like harvesting, though Slip cannot decide which. A frog, out of place and far from water, croaks an omen of which Slip takes note.

The birds have quieted to idle chatter and the sun has nearly reached its zenith when Slip stops along the edge of the Unwood.

The skull is so much smaller than the looming spectre of mortality. And its shape is categorically human.

Slip knows that a human body has 206 bones and that there are far more amassed here in the Unwood. Some of the bones are like trees, cracked open by lightning. Some look more like rocks fallen from a height and fractioned on impact. Their count runs into the thousands.

Assembling the bones should be like putting together a jigsaw puzzle but instead it is like trying to build a house from raw forest. Anatomy textbooks in the library offer Slip blueprints of the human body but do not explain how to fell a tree for lumber or pour a cement foundation. On their own, the bones cannot snap together to form a skeleton. The connective tissue that would hold them is decayed, lost to scavengers and soil. Slip tries to envision muscle and ligament, holds the bones next to living human flesh to see whether they correspond, but there is too much that is missing. Not everything can be imagined.

Some of the bones that are still whole seem to manifest in fours. This could mean that Slip is confusing likeness for identity. This could also mean that there is more than one corpse in the Unwood.

Slip decides that it is better to presume a plurality than a singularity. If there is only one dead person, surely they will not mind the largesse of being addressed as if they contain multitudes. If there is more than one dead person, then they will each appreciate being recognized. Interpellated.

So the bones become The Corpses and Slip begins to speak to them, using the same voice ordinarily reserved to call upon the deer, a soft and thoughtful tone to keep such harmless, gentle kith from startling.

BEAR

Euphoria is a small town, so it still has one video rental store. Euphoria is such a small town that it has only ever had one video rental store. Standing at the cash register behind the glass counter that displays the scenic covers of special release movies and a brigade of posed action figures, Fir—who is average in most discernible ways and softening with middle age—often looks like a drooping background mannequin in a museum exhibit.

The store is called Utopia Video. On Fir's first day of work many years earlier, the store owner had explained, "I was going to call it Euphoria Video, but then my friend said that made it sound like we were selling adult films and I had to change it."

Fir nodded in agreement, but privately thought that Utopia Video was a worse name, the kind a person would give to a religious shop with a conversion mission. "Utopia means no place," Fir had said, not knowing what else to say.

"Oh, we've got a linguist here," the store owner smirked.

"We had to read about it in high school," Fir replied apologetically.

As the years went by, however, Fir began to think that Utopia was in fact the perfect name for a video rental store in a town that seemed displaced in both space and time. Euphoria: an idle town built on fertile soil. The four seasons change continually but the basic form of the town does not. Cozily harbored from the rest of the world by vast swaths of surrounding forest, farmland, and freshwater lakes, Euphoria is forever buffering culturally and technologically, decades behind the progress of the nearest cosmopolitan centres. The metropolises are a few hours' ride by car or by the inter-city bus that runs twice daily, once in the morning and once at night, between Euphoria and everywhere else, except of course on Sundays. Distance mutes signals. Even the blockbusters persistently arrive a year late to Utopia and the closest the store actually gets to adult films is some tender-hearted softcore from the late twentieth century, that last arcadian decade before internet porn took hold of clandestine fantasy.

For most of Fir's tenure at Utopia Video, the shop has had a quiet, dusty feel to it, even when freshly cleaned. But for the past year—ever since two people Fir knew had gone missing—working at the store has been more interesting than ever before. Each customer doubles as a suspect in the disappearance. Fir scrutinizes their rings for signs of recent cleaning, examines their shoes for neglected stains, and glances covertly into their opened wallets for IDs that are not their own as they extract credit cards and cash.

There had been a close call about eight months ago, late at night, right before Fir was about to close up. A customer, thick as a stone pillar, came into the store with jeans covered in dark smudges.

"Painting?" Fir asked casually, evergreen-flecked eyes fixed inexorably on the customer's knees.

"Butchering," the customer said. Blood drained from Fir's face. The customer saw it and clarified, as if to a child: "Butchering *cows.*"

"Oh!" Fir said, and laughed the way people do when their nervous energy has nowhere else to go.

Nothing of concern has happened at the video store since that night.

Until two teenagers, limber and sprightly, wander in amidst the emptiness of this Thursday evening. They are typical lollygaggers in dirty sneakers and hooded sweatshirts, only differentiable insofar as one of them is several inches taller than the other. Fir does not say anything, not even to ask if they need help finding a film, but watches the kids closely, under the pretense of making sure that the young suspects aren't stashing shop merchandise in their backpacks.

The kids go to the horror movie section, which Fir regards as the second-most suspicious section of the store, right after the true crime documentary shelves. The kids seem as indifferent to Fir as they are to the popcorn machine, which is exactly as Fir would have it.

The taller kid picks up two movies and shows their covers to the shorter kid.

"You have to be one of these monsters," the taller kid says. "Which is it gonna be?"

"Ugh," the shorter kid replies, looking from one movie to the other. "I guess the one with fewer scabs."

"Fewer scabs but more hair," the taller kid points out. The shorter kid shrugs.

"Would you rather date a poltergeist," the shorter kid asks in return, holding up two more movies, "or an animate skeleton?"

Fir struggles to focus on their conversation. The kids are loud enough—in fact, they seem unaware of how unnecessarily loud they are—but Fir is immediately bored by their inconsequential chatter. Teenagers, Fir surmises, probably all seem the same to people who are middle-aged and without children of their own to care for, people for whom adolescence is a vestige of their past, a homeland to which they will never return.

"Can you even touch poltergeists?" the taller kid asks.

"I dunno. They must be able to touch you though, right? If they can move furniture," the shorter kid replies.

"I'd date the poltergeist, I guess, who at least has impressive powers. A walking skeleton just seems like half a human."

"That's true." The shorter kid puts the cases back on the shelves.

"Hey," the taller kid says, a bit quieter and more sombre than before, looking intently toward the shorter kid, who has started moving slowly down the row of shelves, oblivious to the creeping seriousness of their conversation. The taller kid presses on. "Speaking of, like, skeletons…"

"Let's get this one," the shorter kid interrupts. "Listen: *A group of teens discover what seems to be a corpse in the local recluse's basement when they enter the house on a dare. Now the neighbourhood psychopath is out to get them and they'll have to use all their wits to keep from being killed before they can figure out how to prove to the cops that they're telling the truth about the body they saw. Little do they know… the corpse was not a corpse and their neighbour is actually a vampire!*"

"Cool, yeah," the taller kid monotones. "So, what I was trying to say—"

"Or what about this one! *Zombie rabbits have taken over a small town and the children are delighted—there's not a vegetable left to eat!*"

"Malapert! Can you listen for one second?" the taller kid hisses. Feet motionless, the shorter kid's head pivots warily sideways, baffled eyes peering back toward where the taller kid stands furiously still.

"What's wrong with *you?*"

"I have something fucking important to tell you, Mal," the taller kid says solemnly and forcefully. Malapert, who evidently goes by Mal under ordinary circumstances, finally turns fully around to face the other, still looking confused.

"Okay, Limn," Mal says. Limn must be the name of the taller kid, Fir decides. "What?"

"You know that person in the trailer park who's really small and really old? Like probably the oldest in the whole park?"

"Yeah…"

"So I was walking around the park by myself the other day, nothing to do, just completely bored—"

Without noticing it, Fir stops mechanically polishing the glass countertop and is instead fossilized in place, listening intently.

"You can't judge me," Limn adds, peering down at Mal with pleading eyes.

"Sure," Mal agrees.

"No, promise me you won't."

"Oh, come on. I'm not judgmental."

"You are."

"Am not."

"Then promise."

"Fine, I promise."

"Well, sometimes, when people aren't home, I look in their windows."

"Really?"

"You said you wouldn't—"

"This better be worth all the build up."

"I saw something in the small old person's window."

"Yeah, obviously! What'd you see?"

"I think they were bones," Limn says, staring down meaningfully at Mal. Fir drops the glass-polishing rag to the ground but does not move to pick it up.

"Bones," Mal repeats, nonplussed.

"Human bones," Limn clarifies impatiently.

"What, like the whole skeleton just lying there in the trailer?"

"No, like a pile of bones sticking out of the top of a backpack."

"How do you know it wasn't just a couple of bones? How do you know they were human bones?"

"I don't know for sure but they *seemed* human."

"Okay. Right, okay. Did you tell anyone else?"

"No, just you."

"Are you going to tell anyone else?"

"Maybe? Do you think I should?"

"You could?"

"Who should I tell? Who would you tell?"

"My parents, probably."

"What about the police?"

"I dunno. I guess I'd see what my parents thought first."

"Hmm."

The kids continue their slow shuffle through the aisles, but they do not talk anymore. Fir retrieves the dropped rag, places it on a shelf of the cabinet next to the cash register, grabs a stack of movies that had been returned earlier, and begins sluggishly ambling through the aisles of the shop floor, restocking the shelves.

Fir reflects on the progress of the situation so far. Limn said that the bones were in a trailer. There are two trailer parks in Euphoria— the nearer one on the edge of the suburbs and the farther one on the border between farms and forest. Euphoria is a cheap place to stop on the way to larger tourist cities. The trailer parks make most of their money renting out camping spots short-term to a slew of seasonal clientele, but also have a selection of long-term residents on account of the town's lack of apartments. Euphoria had made a slow transition from village to town during an era when the detached single-family home, or townhouse when required, was still the dominant residential option everywhere but in the big cities. The latter twentieth-century boom in condos and ultra-high-rise apartment buildings had skipped Euphoria entirely on the way to more populous regions. While sliding the movies back onto their shelves, Fir devises both a plan and a backup plan to find out which trailer park the kids live in. The first plan is to draw out their stay for as long as possible, and engage the kids in conversation, no matter how banal or seemingly irrelevant, to increase the chances the kids will say something that gives them away.

When the kids arrive at the counter with their chosen films, Fir ambles as slowly as possible back to the cash register, drawling, "Be riiight with you."

Finally in place, Fir thumbs through the cases, then taps demonstratively on the last with a blunt, decisive fingernail.

"You don't want this one."

"Why not?" Mal asks. A lock of hair, spiralled and tangled as Spanish moss, has sprung stubbornly free of Mal's hood.

"You're wasting your money. It plays on cable every week."

The kids look at each other. It occurs to Fir that teenagers probably don't watch much cable TV anymore.

"What do you recommend, then?" Limn, whose bugging eyes and long, gangling legs are, more than anything, reminiscent of a stick insect, inquires.

"Glad you asked," Fir says, meandering back to the stocked shelves as painstakingly as a tired seal through heavy sand.

The kids do not follow.

"This here," Fir declares upon returning minutes later.

"What's it about?" Mal asks.

"Someone witnesses a murder but decides not to report it and then is haunted by the victim's ghost," Fir answers, which is a liberal interpretation of the movie's basic premise.

The kids look at each other again. Fir might be imagining their eyes narrowing.

"Yeah, okay," Mal says with a casualness so flippant it sounds forced. Limn stares carefully at Fir, as if searching for confirmation of subtext.

"Great. Can I interest you in some refreshments to accompany your film?" Fir has miscalculated a solicitous tone and realizes there is nothing to do except proceed as if this interaction is entirely normal. "Popcorn?" The teenagers shake their heads. "Pretzels?" Shake. "Black licorice?" Shake. "Red licorice?" Shake. "Soda? We have orange, cola, root beer, cream—"

"We're good, thanks," Mal interjects.

"All right, then, just the movie." Fir is nervous and glances at the kids, who are unreadable. "Three movies. Old releases. That'll be $10.50 for two nights. Let's see how much it'll be for five nights." Fir pulls out a calculator despite already knowing that it will be $15.30.

"We only need them for two nights," Limn says.

"Are you sure? The longer you keep them, the more of a discount there is."

"Two nights is enough," Mal reiterates.

"All right then, three movies for two nights," Fir confirms. "Do you have an account with us?"

"Yes," Limn answers.

"What name is it under?"

Limn spells it out.

"Phone number?"

Limn recites it.

"Postal code?" Fir asks, face solidifying into an expression of indifference.

Limn gives it. Success. Fir speeds through the rest of the transaction like a character in a film being fast-forwarded.

"Thank you for visiting Utopia enjoy your movies come again anytime." Fir shoves the plastic bag full of movies toward the kids and beams in a way that could be mistaken for graciousness. With any luck, the kids will chalk up any strangeness that evening to another instance of adults' enigmatic ways.

Once the kids have left the store, Fir looks up the addresses of Euphoria's two trailer parks and matches the postal code Limn gave to the park north of the downtown. Fir stands illuminated for a moment by the store's fluorescent lights and the flush of success, before blanching, realizing that the trailer park must have dozens of trailers and the postal code will do nothing to distinguish them.

By the time Fir rushes out of the store, through the parking lot, to the road, the kids are nowhere in sight. It has been one year since the disappearance—if Fir's loss was a child it would be on its feet talking by now. But Fir feels the pang of loss, gut-deep, as if it were just being born.

FIZZ

Occasionally, very occasionally, perhaps so occasionally that it may be called rare, people decide they are in love at exactly the same moment. Our two lovers, Culver and Blue, were more normal than that.

Culver, the first lover, only had to meet Blue twice to know what was happening. Blue, the second lover, reciprocated far more slowly, treading long stretches of time. But once dipped beneath the water, Blue grew gills. A fish for life. A reversal of evolution that could not be undone.

Time is the only gift greater than space that we can give to one another. Culver brought all the clocks on earth to Blue and they drew them into the sea. Hands stopped and their minutes together descended into a fathomless dark.

The first time the lovers met it was by accident at a house party. Blue was effervescent, clouded by a fizz of prosecco and fresh desire, spilling secret after secret to someone whose face could not afterwards be recalled. Blue told this acquaintance about their latest infatuation, someone named Culver,

"That strange name again," the acquaintance said. "I swear I just met a Culver earlier tonight."

"I don't think Culver's here," Blue muttered, glancing about nervously.

"It has to be the same person," the acquaintance gasped. "How many people can there be in this town named Culver?"

"Forget I brought it up." Blue made a hushing motion.

"Culver!" The acquaintance, tipsy and full of misdirected enthusiasm, shouted into the crowd.

A drawn figure, overdressed in black silk slacks, appeared at the acquaintance's side. "Yes?"

"Aha!" The acquaintance clapped once. "I think you two know each other."

Culver turned, lingering for a moment on Blue's out-of-place, two-toned saddles shoes and matching black jacket with white lapels, and smiled. "Do we?"

"We do not," Blue said flatly.

"This isn't your Culver?" the acquaintance asked Blue.

"No," Blue replied.

"You have a Culver?" Culver interjected, grin spreading.

"I don't have a Culver, I know a Culver. Not you. A different Culver."

"Two Culvers!" the acquaintance marvelled. "Imagine that."

Since Blue and Culver hardly knew anyone else at the party, they stayed side by side even once the acquaintance left for another drink and never returned. They flirted for an hour before drifting off to dally with other people because they both felt young that night, so much younger than they were.

By morning, they had both sunk back into the hollows of their eye sockets and wished then for each other's phone number.

One accident is a mistake but two accidents is fate. Blue and Culver met again, happenstance, on a street corner. Blue led them into a store full of antiques, where they found a vanity mirror stained with painted harebells that neither of them could bear to part with.

The lovers had spoken to each other every day since then. They scattered words like petals, or dreams, beneath one another's feet.

MAP OF MISDEEDS

It had been three months and 11 days since Fir stopped being able to say for certain that the lovers were still alive.

Fir was sitting cross-legged and staring at a map of the town that was laid out on the floor of Fain's bedroom. "We've talked to the police. We've driven the streets. We've been through the neighbourhood all the way up to their door. Now we need to get inside," Fir said.

Fain nodded. "The longer we wait to go to the house, the greater the risk that it'll be sold or demolished before we have time to search it," Fain agreed. Fain was sitting on a faded swivel chair, which had a worn-out cylinder so the seat of the chair existed in permanent close proximity to the ground.

"They had enough money that I bet the mortgage is still getting paid," Fir said. "But eventually they'll owe somebody for something and the bank will end up repossessing the house."

"Probably, yeah. Especially if they never show up."

"Right."

"I mean—"

"It's okay. I understand that I might not see them again. Not alive anyways." Fir chose not to breathe, for it seemed more composed than a sigh. "When should we go?"

"If we went at night, there would be less chance of us being seen, but our actions would probably seem more suspicious if we were unlucky enough to be discovered."

"It'll be easier to search with daylight rather than flashlights."

"That's another consideration."

"I think daytime is the way to go." Fir looked to the window, from which the cool, dimming wash of twilit sky seeped over the room. "We can't go today, then."

Fain looked to the clock. "Yeah. Not today."

"Tomorrow maybe?" Fir asked.

"Working," Fain replied. "Overmorrow?"

"Sure, we'll go *overmorrow,*" Fir said with a slightly arch inflection. Fain gazed steadily at Fir, disaffected, either not recognizing or preferring not to acknowledge the tease. Fir coughed delicately. "We'll need a plausible excuse in case we're caught."

"We could tell the truth," Fain said, apparently in earnest.

"I'm not sure how sympathetic the police would be. *Sorry for breaking the law, it's just that we thought you were doing such a shit job we decided we'd better take over.* You know?"

"Okay, yeah, you're right. Did they have pets? We could pretend to be entirely concerned about animal welfare."

"If they had pets, I would have gone in already! But I'm pretty sure all they would have are plants."

"I guess impending plant death doesn't carry the same kind of urgency. Not yet, anyways. Maybe if they keep doing those studies on plant consciousness…" Fain was staring through the window while speaking, as if looking out into another world. "Wait, what if it wasn't their plants but your plants and they'd just been looking after the plants and you were going to retrieve the plants, which are really important to you, maybe rare orchids or something, your investment plants, and you're breaking in because you're protecting your money. That's the kind of thing authority figures can sympathize with."

"There are two problems, one being that we don't actually have expensive orchids to plant at the scene to justify our excuse and the other being that I don't look like the sort of person who invests in anything." Fir hooked a finger through a split shoulder-seam.

"Not all rich people look rich."

"But all poor people look poor."

"I don't think—"

"Let's just not get caught. How much trouble can we get in for trespassing? We won't even be stealing anything."

"Depends on whether you have to smash a window or break down a door to get in. Of course we won't because I'll have my lockpicking kit."

"Why do you have a lockpicking kit?"

"Previous career," Fain said. "Wayward youth."

Fir stared and Fain stared back. Fir considered asking for elaboration but decided against it, because Fain might have been joking. Fain continued, "Are you sure you don't know anyone who was close enough to them to maybe have a key? This would be so much easier if someone could just let us in."

"That's the problem. I wasn't close enough to them to know who else would have been close to them." Fir resumed staring at the ground, making sure to gaze in the general direction of the map, as a pretext, so Fain would not suspect that melancholy might be the cause of the staring. The map offered plausible deniability, which Fir felt was always important to keep tucked in one's back pocket in any situation where one was vulnerable.

Like keeping spare change in one's wallet for an emergency bus ride or bit of food.

A cacophony downstairs interfered with their momentary quiet.

"I didn't know you had a dog in the house," Fir said, guessing at the cause of the sharp juts of noise.

"We don't. That's one of my roommates. Laughing, I think."

"Really? Which roommate?"

"A new one. You haven't met."

"A nice one?"

"Better than the most recently departed."

"The one who was always trying to talk to me when I came over?"

"Yeah. And forever trying to come into my room and chat. Not threatening, just no sense of boundaries. I was a grown adult paying rent and I had to lock my door, turn off my light, and pretend I was asleep or away just to have some peace." Fain's voice was so level it was a straight line, like the end of an electrocardiograph. Fir recognized the sound, a collapse of verve, having heard it once before while Fain was laid up with a broken leg.

"I'm glad you got a replacement."

"Ha. I didn't have much say. None of us did. The homeowner finds them and sends them in and we have to get used to a new stranger."

"Oh, I didn't realize. I thought you and your roommates got together and voted on somebody."

"We used to, until a pick of ours dipped out without paying. Then the homeowner took over. That's how we ended up with the eternal conversationalist. Anyways, whatever, drama, right? Let's get back to our planning. We still don't have a reason for being in the house."

"We can say I wanted to check and make sure nothing was wrong inside. I haven't heard from the two of them, maybe they have a good excuse for being away even, but it seems like no one is monitoring the house itself. I started worrying after that heavy rain we got the other day that there might be flooding in their basement. It didn't seem like enough of an emergency to involve the police, so we just went in on our own."

"I guess that's the best we have. It's not a very smart excuse though, so we'll have to really make it sound like we're unintelligent. Two bumbling, meddlesome do-gooders who aren't possibly clever enough to pull one over on the police."

"You mean we have to insult our intelligence so we don't insult theirs?"

"Something like that."

"All right." Fir stood up, wriggling a stiff neck and shoulders loose. "I'm so tired."

Fain, face softening, seemed to understand the endlessness of that word. Tired. Deflated. Empty as a flat tire.

"We'll find something in the house. I'm sure of it."

"Thanks for everything," Fir said with a tight, faint smile. "I don't know how I could do this without you."

"Yeah, so I've heard." Fain smiled, rising and walking after Fir toward the bedroom door. They both stopped on the threshold and Fain put a hand on Fir's shoulder. "Now go home and sleep, you're getting sentimental."

BLUEPRINTS

In the dinette of the travel trailer, the trailer which is home, home where Slip never speaks aloud, the kettle is shrieking, forcing a jet of steam through the shrill, pursed mouth of its spout. Sitting on the single chair pulled up to the foldout table, Slip assesses the space, considers whether it would permit a second chair, a prospective bit of furniture that had for so long seemed neither a useful necessity nor a pleasing luxury. What would Slip do with two chairs? Use them on alternating days?

FIRST TIME

Three months and 13 days had passed since the lovers disappeared from Fir's life.

"Let's not take the car." That was the first thing Fain said when Fir arrived. "We'll walk. I don't want anyone to track my license plate, even if we do have a perfectly respectable reason for breaking into the house."

"That makes sense," Fir, the hapless lamb, agreed and they left on foot, side by side. Fain, the cheerful and diligent herding dog, set the pace, efficient but not suspiciously swift.

It was mid-morning on a weekday and they were headed toward the suburbs. A car passed them by every few minutes. Birds, perched on tree limbs or rooftops, chirped intermittently in the middle distance. Now and then Fir and Fain gave the sidewalk over to a lone parent with a stroller or an old couple holding hands and Fain watched them studiously, or enviously. The sidewalk ended when they reached the suburbs and they had to continue by strolling on the side of the road, through the streets repeatedly looping back on themselves, bypassing the dead ends and culs-de-sac where the most intimidatingly large houses resided, destinations in themselves, not stopover points on thoroughfares leading somewhere else.

"So you've never broken into a house before," Fain said declaratively, and Fir felt no need to reply. "That's funny. I've always thought of you as a take-what-you-can-get type."

"Oh really? Why's that?"

"You like movies, so you work at the video store, probably because it's the easiest job you could get in the field. You live in an apartment by yourself because you can basically afford to and you don't want to fuss too much with other people." The apartment to which Fain referred was the converted upper floor of a convenience store. "You have some hobbies. You read plays and scripts, you practice guitar regularly. Yet you don't try out for theatre productions, you don't join a band or book shows. You don't treat anything in your life seriously. You take what you can get, instead of reaching for what you could have if you tried harder. Nothing you do is a labour of love because you don't love labour."

Fir stopped walking and looked at Fain. From anyone else's mouth, that kind of affected presumptuousness would have been insulting, but because it came from Fain, Fir received it with only a flicker of impatience. Fir and Fain had been friends for several years, having met at Reel Time, Euphoria's small-town take on a cinema, which had persevered in a local book and comic shop's basement. It could hold 20 people at its most capacious and its screen was roughly the size of an average classroom's PVC projector screen. The film showing that night, a modern Gothic classic from Australia, was already 35 years old by the time of its debut in Euphoria. The cinema did have a genuine popcorn machine, though, which filled the theatre with the ersatz-butter scent of coconut oil and seasoned salt, and the cinema's owner would look the other way when patrons sipped from flasks stashed in their jacket pockets.

Fir and Fain had scarcely anything in common, save for their

love of film and a stubborn sense of loyalty to their friends, of which
Fir had few. Still, Fir would devotedly show up whenever summoned,
even if they hadn't spoken to one another in years. Fain, by contrast,
was a cardinal flower among hummingbirds. People flocked around
Fain. There had always been a profusion of applicants when a room
in the house Fain rented with several friends became available.
Lovers flitted in and out of Fain's life on a near-constant basis.
And yet, Fain was somehow always available, always able to make
time for anyone who needed it, which, right then, was Fir.

"Why do you think we're doing all this work, *detective?*"
Fir asked. It was a sarcastic question, but without malice. "Spending
countless hours searching for the two of them even when no one
else is?"

"Oh, I didn't mean to imply that you didn't—"

"I know."

"I'm sorry."

"You don't have to be sorry. I'm not trying to call you out. I just
think you should remember why we're doing this."

"I guess I thought you were just doing the right thing. Being
decent. Under the circumstances."

"Well, hopefully we're doing that, too. But…"

"But we wouldn't be here," Fain said with a nod, seeming
to appreciate for the first time the true seriousness of the situation,
"if you hadn't loved—"

"If I didn't *love,*" Fir interrupted. "Present tense. They're missing.
Let's try not to talk about them like they're dead."

Love. Was it even fair for Fir to call it that? Blue had said
it was the wrong word, and Fir had protested. What other word
was there for years of indefatigable devotion? Well, maybe it was not
love. Maybe Fir was just clinging like a stranded creature to a tiny

island sinking into the water.

"Of course," Fain said. "You're right."

"I'm sorry," Fir sighed. "I don't know why I'm snapping at you."

"You're worried. It's been a hard few months for you since they disappeared. I'm here to help," Fain said. "Even when you annoy me."

Fain started walking again and Fir followed. The sun glared down at them, a single judgmental eye. Fir thought it very inconsiderate of the sky to not at least offer a few modest clouds on such a grave occasion requiring considerable discretion.

"Have I also told you how much I appreciate you?" Fir asked finally, to ease the tension.

"Yes, every time you see me," Fain replied. "It makes it easier to forgive your irritability."

"I really am grateful."

"You're my friend." Fain shrugged. "And it's not like there's much else to get up to in this town," Fain added with a wink that was probably for Fir's benefit. "How many free movies do you think I can get out of this?"

"Probably as many as you want for as long as I have my job."

"Which you've had for, remind me, how long?" Fain asked. Fir had to do arithmetic to remember.

"Going on 21 years. Thanks for asking. I feel old now, and awfully dull after that drab summary you provided of my life." Though self-deprecating, Fir made the remarks sociably, with a bleat of laughter.

"I don't think you're dull," Fain said.

"Just tolerably respectable and wholly unambitious."

"You misunderstand me. I admire people who try to lead a good, simple life."

"That's me, pure as salt and light, committing only slight offences against etiquette and the province." Evasively, Fir had taken on a cinematic, extravagant tone that obscured sincere emotion and betrayed an adolescence spent in a high school theatre; the theatre in fact, was one of only two things from youth that Fir missed. In Fir's adult life, watching films had largely occupied the time that might have been reserved for maintaining a well-rounded circle of friends and peers. "Yes, my transgressions are trivial. Except," Fir paused ominously, "for the single carnal crime that has cast a shadow over my entire life these past two seasons."

"You shouldn't be so hard on yourself," Fain replied, earnestly. "What you did was questionable, sure, but because of it we're out here right now searching for people who might be very glad to be found."

"That remains to be seen."

The house they sought looked nothing like the scene of a tragedy; it was as prim and placid as every other house in the neighbourhood when they approached. Set back from the road by a sizeable driveway and an upward-rolling lawn, it was an augmented Cape Cod, grey-bricked, with two white-framed Georgian windows on each side of a taciturn navy door, and twin dormers like frank eyes on a plain and open facade. The windowpanes were visibly fogged, even at a slight distance, as if they had not been cleaned for several months, though Fir felt that no conclusions could be drawn from that. People get busy, preoccupied. Glass cleaning is not always a top priority.

"You'd think they'd gone out of town for the month," Fir said, stopping at the foot of the stone steps that led up to a wide, flat stoop, and observing that the mailbox was full but not overflowing.

"Maybe they have," Fain suggested gently.

"I guess we should knock. Just in case."

Fir climbed the steps, forcefully thrust the black wrought-iron knocker against the door, stood back, and checked the time.

"I'll knock again," Fir said after precisely one minute had elapsed.

"Good idea," Fain replied encouragingly.

Fir knocked again, and then, restless, not knowing how long it would be appropriate to wait, began to glance about. There were no chairs on the stoop. The only decorative gestures were two large, ornamental pots holding tall, scarlet gladioli that appeared to be in blossoming good health.

"I don't think they're answering," Fir noted unecessarily.

"Seems not," Fain agreed. "Let's go to the back. You go around the left side of the house, I'll go around the right."

They parted. Fir observed that the windows on the left side of the house were too high and small to climb into, but the backyard was mercifully surrounded and concealed by a high cypress hedge that wanted trimming. The wooden deck, painted a crisp white, held only two charcoal-grey Adirondack chairs and led to a hospitable sliding glass door.

"Doesn't look like they host a lot of garden parties," Fain commented, emerging from the far side of the house.

"No, I don't think they're the type," Fir said. "Did you see anything?"

"Nothing of interest," Fain answered. "Nice private yard though. Keep watch anyways and let me know if anyone's coming. I'm going to get this back door open."

Fir's gaze remained carefully averted as Fain took out the lockpicking kit. Perhaps Fain had been apprenticed to the art of lockpicking while training to be a security guard. Then again, perhaps the job was merely a course correction for a young person veering wayward, and in that drift Fain learned how to outsmart a lock. In either case, Fir felt that to look just then would be to watch Fain undress, revealing a secret self that could neither be wholly hidden nor should be wholly known.

"Let me know when you're done," Fir said.

"You can look," Fain responded. "You might learn something."

Fir did not look.

The door slid open. Fain waved a hand graciously toward it. "You should go in first."

"It occurs to me," Fir said, standing on the threshold, "that this will be my first time inside the house." The words ached out loud.

"Really?"

"I've been as far as the porch. Back when they were, you know, around."

"Back when you were welcome but also not welcome."

"Yeah. Persona semi-grata." Fir inhaled, stepped through the door, and stood at the edge of what was obviously the living room.

"Do you want us to take off our shoes?" Fain asked, entering and standing beside Fir.

"I guess not," Fir said, glancing down. "Burglars don't take off their shoes, do they?"

"No, but if they're smart they throw them out after." Fain closed the sliding door behind them.

"I'll keep that in mind." Fir began to circle the room. Bare white couches. A sheepskin rug in front of a stone hearth. A television set, attached to the opposite wall, so sleek in its design that it looked more like a simulacrum of itself than a functioning appliance. The fuzz of dust on its screen bespoke disuse.

"Hardwood." Fain tapped a soled foot on the floor.

"I didn't know you cared about that kind of thing."

"Everyone likes a good hardwood, don't they?"

"Sure. I suppose so," Fir said. Guess after guess, never a certainty.

Fir led them out of the living room.

"Anything you think we should be looking for?" Fain asked.

"Fuck. I have no idea. A note? A journal? An itinerary?"

"Okay. How about we just stay together and we'll discuss anything of interest we might come across."

"Yeah, alright." Fir started to move off in the direction of the adjoining kitchen.

"But also we should keep an eye out for open maps, wallets, keys, and computer passwords. And let's take photos of the rooms, to reconsider later."

"Makes sense."

"And I see you've forgotten your gloves so maybe try not to touch or move anything and if you do pick something up you should do it with your sleeves and put it back precisely where you found it."

"I'll try to remember all of that."

Fir and Fain moved haltingly through the house, twitching when they heard the voices of neighbours or the calls of birds. Fain photographed unwashed dishes in the kitchen sink, spoiled steak in the refrigerator, an empty shoe mat and full coat pegs by the front door.

"Who leaves their jackets at home unless they expect to return?" Fir wondered aloud while Fain delicately patted down the pockets and pulled out a wallet.

"Cash. Credit card. Driver's license." Fain turned to Fir, who could not speak. "Let's check the garage."

There were two cars, a cerise import convertible and a pearl-blue coupe.

"How many cars did they have?" Fain asked. Throat thick with bile, Fir coughed before answering.

"Two?" A long pause. "Probably two." Fir dredged for the right memory. "Blue and I used to ride in the coupe." That phrasing, a little wishful, a little wistful, made it sound as if Fir and Blue did it regularly, but it had only happened a handful of times. "And just before they went missing, I saw Culver standing in the driveway beside the convertible. They definitely had these two cars. But there might have been others." Fir's eyes swept the floor and fixed on a dark stain.

Fain noticed. "That's not blood. It's just oil." Fir seemed unconvinced. "My car had a bad oil leak once. The whole floor of our carport turned that colour," Fain added reassuringly. Fir still didn't move. "There could be a second wallet," Fain pointed out. "They could have gotten a ride to the train station, or taken a cab to the airport. The cars not being gone doesn't tell us anything definite." Fir nodded, a nod that was all defeat, and sat down on the cement.

Some 20 years ago—before Culver, before the coupe— Blue, like Fir, had a bicycle. A vintage, pumpkin-bright single-speed with cruiser bars. One weekend, Fir had booked off time from Utopia Video and ridden the train out of town to take campus tours of the two universities closest to Euphoria, both of which were an hour or more away. Late on Sunday night, Fir's return train arrived back in Euphoria. A physically and psychologically exhausted Fir shouldered a heavy backpack, and descended the steps of the train, dreading the long, dejected walk home. The tours had been failures. Both campuses had filled Fir with a sense of foreboding. Their austere buildings held less charm than banks. The laboriously cheerful student reps conducting the tours seemed like heralds of bureaucratic performativity rather than wisdom. Education, that great abstraction that Fir had hoped to leap upon like the gleaming deck of a grand ship, felt instead like a mere expansion of the dullest portions of the town Fir wanted to leave.

That Sunday night, Euphoria's tiny train station—situated inconveniently far from downtown so that the tracks could bypass most of the city infrastructure—was empty. The ticket booth had closed an hour before and Fir was the only disembarking passenger from a train that had hurriedly sped along to its next destination. Fir tightened a shoelace and started walking.

Trudging the single road that led from the station to downtown, Fir passed the long line of closely crowded, strawberry-box bungalows with their dull ivory siding. The evening hummed with the corona discharge of power lines, and with mosquitoes swarming the houses' bare amber bulbs that dimly lit the concrete porches the size of milk crates. It was a sight Fir had seen a hundred times before, and it usually connoted nothing in particular, but that night it was immensely depressing. *This is all there is,* Fir thought. *There is nothing better somewhere else.*

Into this landscape of glum reflections, there came a flaring balefire of orchid light. Small at first, it grew in size as it moved closer, until it filled Fir's entire field of vision.

"Blue," Fir said as the bicycle squeaked to a stop. "What are you doing here? I wasn't expecting you."

"You told me you were getting in on the last train," Blue explained, hopping off the bike and letting it fall onto the road in the hurry of getting to Fir. "I missed you." Blue's whole body folded Fir into a hold so complete it was like being underwater. "Let's go," Blue said, releasing Fir, who gulped down a mouthful of cool night air. Blue picked up the bike and patted the wide curve of the handlebars. "Get on."

When Fir tried to assess that event objectively, it seemed obvious that it was a completely ordinary encounter between two people. And yet, decades later, sitting on the floor of Blue and

Culver's garage, Fir still thought of those few seconds as one of life's scarce glimpses of paradise, when what one wanted and what one had were exactly the same thing. Did Blue remember it the same? Did Blue remember it at all?

Fain pulled Fir back like a boat whose docking line had broken loose. "No, come on, don't do that." Fain, whose lower spine was the only weak point on a frame as low to the ground and powerful as a pack pony, refrained from trying to haul Fir up by the wrists, and instead waited for the pleading tone to do its work. Fir continued to stare morosely at the floor. "You can have a meltdown later. Get back on your feet," Fain commanded with half-hearted severity, before walking over to a row of tote boxes on the back wall and appealing to Fir's generosity instead. "Help me check these. We might find something useful."

They found: unopened bottles of antifreeze and windshield washer fluid, a tin of wax, a nearly-empty bag of plant fertilizer, a pair of dirt-smudged gardening gloves, a trowel, hedge trimmers, strings of multicoloured lights, two paint roller brushes, and a can with a petrified drip of paint running down its side.

"We should check the trunks of their cars." Fir was grim.

"I'll do it," Fain said decisively and went to get the keys.

"No bodies," Fain reported, after closing the second trunk. "No clues."

There was nothing of significance on the rest of the ground floor either, not in the dining room, nor in the guest bathroom. Fir and Fain stood midway between the ascending and descending staircases.

"Which way?" Fir asked.

"Let's just get the basement over with," Fain suggested.

The basement was far less unnerving than others of its ilk. It had light grey carpet and white drywall that could have easily shown stains but did not. There was no ramshackle root cellar or low-ceilinged furnace room or water damage creeping up the walls. Like the garage, it held neatly-packed tote boxes full of sundries and holiday decorations.

"No bodies," Fain said with strained relief as they left.

"No bodies," Fir echoed.

The upper floor was a half-storey. A hallway connected four rooms: a master bedroom with an ensuite bath, a guest bedroom, and what appeared at a glance to be two personal rooms. The master bedroom and the guest room were plucked straight from furniture stores. They were finely outfitted with king-sized beds and high-thread-count cotton duvets, and devoid of idiosyncrasy. Night tables with reading lamps bookended the beds but bore no books. One table held a glass of water in which a spider had drowned. Dressers contained folded clothes and extra towels. Sunrays became a delicate haze through the filter of chiffon curtains.

Entering the master bedroom's ensuite was like walking into a hotel bathroom. Necessities came in singles. One bar of soap for the sink, one bar of soap and one bottle of shampoo for the bath, still ever so lightly ringed with scum, one hand towel hanging on a rack. In the medicine cabinet, there was one bottle of acetaminophen and one ceramic dish filled with cotton balls. Fain checked underneath the sink for loose razor blades, or pills with alarming, esoteric names, but found simple, familiar hydrogen peroxide. The only twins were the toothbrushes, bone dry.

As they stepped out of the bathroom into the hallway, there was a knock at the front door. They stopped moving, looked at each other, waiting for the situation to inevitably escalate or deescalate. Knocks came like thunderclaps and they wondered how far behind the lightning could be.

"Hey! HEY!" Someone was shouting on the porch but the words that followed were indecipherable. Fain began to tiptoe down the stairs toward the sound.

"What are you doing?" Fir hissed, but Fain offered no response. As they moved forward, the words of the person on the porch came clear, like a dial hitting a radio station.

"—every day, every day mind you, and you can't even dignify me with a response, never mind tend to your goddamn yard. I have a lawyer, you know, and I don't want to call my lawyer but I will. Your yard is a disgrace to this whole neighbourhood and I know, *I know,* that a bylaw enforcement officer has come by because there's a notice in your mailbox you haven't even bothered to pick up—"

"What should we do?" Fir whispered nervously to Fain, whose vigorous head shake answered clearly: *Stand still, keep quiet.*

"What if I wanted to sell my house? I ask you. I'd lose ten percent because of your *slov-en-li-ness.* You are compromising property values for the entire street and it's disgusting. Money. That's all you are. You have the money but you have no thought or care for social mores. For time-honoured traditions. Well, I won't stand for it. I will show you and you will see. You. Will. See."

Retreating footsteps echoed with a repressed but increasingly remote fury. The neighbour had presumably been referring to a distant rather than an immediate future, having left the house without showing either Fir or Fain anything. Even after the sound had faded to silence, Fir and Fain stood motionless on the stairs.

"Maybe the police will listen if someone like that reports them missing," Fir said flatly.

"Should we finish what we started? Or are you afraid the neighbour will come back?"

"Let's get it over with as quickly as we can."

The first personal room was noteworthy insofar as it clearly belonged to a single individual but revealed almost nothing of a personality. It spoke to a set of interests. Curio cabinets displayed tasteful glass animals; the walls were partially obscured by a few large, abstract paintings that shared an unidentifiable aesthetic similarity though the signatures all differed; one of the desk drawers contained a small stack of maps. Another desk drawer contained orderly documents, all of which testified to relative financial ease. What the room lacked was any record of private thought. There was no notepad, no personal calendar, no diary, no letters waiting to be sent, no computer, no phone.

"This tells us nothing." Fir sighed.

"Really? I think it tells us quite a lot."

"Like what, for example?"

"Like the fact that this person is hiding something. How can a room *possibly* be so impersonal otherwise?"

Fir snorted involuntarily. Culver, on the few times they had met—before Culver and Blue were entirely subsumed into dating, and later, marriage—had always seemed thoroughly impersonal. Portentous, aloof. Polite in the way a statue could be solemn and respectfully taciturn.

"It's exactly as if they'd cleared the space out. That means they knew what was coming." Fain looked meaningfully at Fir, who could think of nothing to say to that.

The second personal room had an unnecessary number of chairs for any single occupant. Multiple chaise lounges with sweeping curves, a cushioned reading seat by the window, a marshmallow pouf draped in sheer muslin. Fir recognized that it was Blue's room, even before seeing the violin reclined in a stand in the corner. The room, like Blue, was gracefully inviting, if slightly excessive.

An indulgent counterpart to Culver's refined collections. And, just as Blue could become cozily intimate with a person without revealing anything of consequence, this room gave little away. Though the drawers of a lovely antique vanity, complete with a painted mirror, were teeming with personal items—sheet music that was lightly annotated by hand, postcards that were stamped but left blank, laptop accessories without a corresponding computer, a passport due to be renewed, photos of the homeowners when they were young—and though, still more significantly, a stack of letter paper and a fountain pen were prominently displayed on the table of the vanity, which suggested at least a wish to communicate, there was not a single keepsake to confirm that the inhabitant of the room had ever actually expressed anything to anyone. Fir thought that the two rooms, in their elegant, secretive beauty, were a perfect pair.

Without thinking, Fir touched the neck of the violin, and would have sworn the wood still felt warm, as though someone had been playing it just minutes ago.

"What do you make of it?" Fain asked.

"It feels like they're about to walk in on us. At the same time, it's as if they stopped living here ten years ago."

Fir and Fain left the house the way they had entered it. They stood on the deck for a moment before departing.

"What if they're buried in the backyard?" Fir asked.

"Did they wear rings?"

"They used to. Both wore wedding bands, and Culver wore this pompous class ring that always annoyed me."

"Meet me back here tonight just after sunset." Fain began to walk away. "And if anyone asks, you're a landscaper here to offer an estimate for yardwork to fix the place up after such lengthy neglect."

LOCAL LORE

Residents of the area claim the Unwood is one of those rare, liminal spaces where people go to die. Strictly speaking, the Unwood is only somewhat unusual. It is an ordinary glade in an increasingly extraordinary forest—the Carolinian forest—which once sprawled across the eastern side of the continent but whose sensitive ecosystems have been gradually redacted and replaced by pragmatic farms, industry, and houses. Even the tracts of forest that were not specifically cut down have still often succumbed to pollution, invasive species, and dread.

Somehow, though, the forest of the Unwood has continued to bear on, alive or undead, while those around it fall, and its initial, uncanny persistence has become a self-fulfilling prophecy. The Unwood's name is a translation—or possibly a mistranslation—of its first name, which has since been lost along with much of the language from which it came. That language fled in the mouths of people who spoke it once. When the people were forcibly dispossessed, sometimes made to disappear altogether, the words they carried dispersed like dust turned to clouds in a lake. This is one way that language can vanish. It is very different, of course, from people laying down their own words like stones they no longer need.

For millennia, under any of its names, people who have made their homes near the Unwood have regarded the glade and its surrounding forest with a tentative reverence, holding their breath when they get too close to it, as if it were already a graveyard. Proximity makes their hands tremble a little, their heads feel a trifle light, but nowadays the effect is so mild and they are so modern that they laugh it off as susceptibility to superstition, if they mention it to each other at all.

Farmers, however, clasp their almanacs and take no chances, refusing to plant their precious, delicate peach and cherry trees anywhere near the Unwood. Wild berry pickers avoid the fruit of any bushes within three stones' throws of it. Housing developers eschew the area in favour of sunnier, grassier tracts of land that exude life-propelling energy, soothing parents' fears and inviting children's feet. Cynical teenagers, the kind who go looking for the supernatural and dare ghosts to show themselves, tend to think that the Unwood is proof that even urban legends are dull in Euphoria, and so leave it alone, preferring to use the woods closer to town as cover for their late-night bonfires and bottles of vodka stolen from their families' liquor cabinets.

The last unbuilt land standing between downtown and the Unwood was eventually bought by an out-of-towner who paid cash, hired contractors from two cities over to construct a scant infrastructure, and put up a sign declaring the launch of The Singing Frog, officially Euphoria's second, and cheapest, trailer park. Slip was the first to put a deposit on a lot.

During The Singing Frog's sophomore summer, Slip intercepted one of the camping tourists walking down the dead end road that led from the trailer park to the forest.

"You shouldn't go in there," Slip said.

"Why not?" the tourist asked.

"It's a place where people go to die." Slip parroted the accepted phrase.

"Like a suicide forest?" the tourist asked.

Slip's head shook back and forth vehemently. "No, no, no, not at all," Slip remarked disapprovingly. "That's so violent."

"Okay then." The tourist resumed moving toward the forest.

"You're walking into the mouth of a whale," Slip warned, and the tourist stopped again. "A huge, land-locked whale who will swallow you whole. You will sleep forever in the belly of the whale."

"A whale can't even swallow a human being whole," the tourist muttered.

"It's an underworld," Slip said, trying another metaphor. "If you go there, it will be nearly impossible to return to the living."

The tourist finally turned back, perhaps as much to shake off Slip as to escape the looming shadows of the trees.

Years later, after shrinking with age, Slip discovered that some people—people who are small enough, people who are old enough, people who understand that there is no line that marks the start of a forest, only a continuum of landscapes where trees gradually grow sparser or denser, people who know that there is no boundary on earth that can keep life and death apart from each other—can walk into the belly of the whale, stay for a short while, and crawl back out between the plates of its baleen.

THIS IS NOT A SHOVEL

"Hey." Fain's disembodied voice emerged from the shadows of the hedge, making Fir jump like a skittish deer.

"Hey," Fir said. "So. What are we really doing here?"

Fain passed Fir an object with a long handle that appeared at first to be a shovel.

"This is not a shovel," Fir observed, taking the object in hand.

"Correct. It's a metal detector. But I also brought a shovel." Fain paused. "In case we need it."

"Right."

"And I've rethought our cover story. Landscaping doesn't make much sense as an excuse at this hour of the day. If anyone asks, we're just two obnoxious people with a poor sense of boundaries who are looking for buried gold."

"We are."

"Exactly. That's why it's the perfect lie."

They heard three warbling chirps and dug three holes that night. They found: a dime, a paper clip, nothing.

"Either they're not here—" Fir began.

"Or someone took their rings," Fain finished.

Fir and Fain walked away from the house, back toward

the main street, stopping at a corner on the periphery of Euphoria's downtown, where they would normally part ways to head to their respective homes.

"I…can't." Fir's voice was uneven.

"Can't what?" Fain prodded.

"I can't go home right now. I can't face…"

"Yeah."

"I don't know where to go."

"There's that café about a block from here." Fain checked the time. "They're open for another hour or so."

"All right, I'll go there I guess. Thanks for everything tonight."

"I'm obviously going with you."

"You don't have to do that."

"I know."

"I'm sorry. I shouldn't have brought it up. I feel so lost. You should go home, you must be tired."

"Shut up already, I said I'm coming with you." Fain led them forward.

Even the way Fir walked was miserable—hunched shoulders, hands in pockets, eyes on the ground.

"You're a pitiful sight, aren't you?" Fain said. Fir looked up and saw that Fain was grinning tentatively.

"You're mocking me at a time like this?" Fir smiled thinly in return.

"You're a contrarian. It's the only way to get you to stop feeling sorry for yourself."

In the café, Fain pulled out a deck of cards.

"Do you always keep a deck of cards on you?" Fir asked.

"Only for emergencies."

"What kind of emergencies?"

"The kind where you don't want to be alone but it's hard to talk."

"You're better than a therapist, you know."

"You wouldn't know, you've never been to one."

"Maybe I have."

"You definitely haven't."

"Are you mocking me again?"

"No, that time I was complimenting you," Fain said. They played wordlessly for several minutes.

"Did I tell you I got interviewed?" Fir asked.

"No. When was that?"

"Last week. Twice. Sort of."

"Sort of?"

"One was by a reporter for the local paper, doing some kind of story on civilians' opinions of the police. Total coincidence I was chosen. Apparently the police are planning a public consultation in advance of releasing their new budget later this year, and the paper wants to get ahead of it. Anyways, obviously I had some thoughts on how police handle missing persons cases…"

"And the second?"

"Oh, just some local newsmonger with a blog. Didn't interview me, per se. Well okay, didn't even talk to me, but saw my quote in the paper and made a post about it that I came across while doing research. It was hard to get the gist of what the blog's about. I'm still not sure whether it's libertarian raving or just someone with nothing better to do than go to city council meetings and write up critiques."

"A boon for our cause."

They stayed until the café closed and left them stranded again in the night.

"Are you ready to go home yet?" Fain asked as they stood on the sidewalk.

"I should be," Fir said.

"That means you're not," Fain declared and Fir was relieved to be understood without explanation. "Not much is open anymore except bars."

"Right."

"I'm guessing that's not the kind of place you want to be right now, is it?"

"What other choice is there?"

"You haven't had a lot of friends, have you?" The question sounded rhetorical—a dispassionate observation by Fain.

"I've had friends." Fir shrugged.

"Close friends?"

"Apparently not?"

"Okay, here's how this goes: I'm going to invite you to stay with me, because we're friends, and that's the sort of thing friends do for each other when they're having a really bad time. And in the future, you'll have enough sense to tell me when you are having a bad time and want to stay over."

Fir stared with a rare, plaintive look, wishing to be told what to do.

"This is where you say, *Yes, okay,*" Fain supplied.

"Yes, okay."

"Great, come on." Fain walked a half-step ahead, as if it were Fir's first time.

When Fain finally shut the bedroom door against the clamour of the world, Fir sighed and looked for a place to crumple inward. Finding none, Fir stood at odds with the room until Fain drew them both into an inelegant embrace that was as firm and steady as a heavy coat.

"I'm sorry," Fain said over Fir's shoulder. "This never gets easier for you, does it?"

"Not really." Fir's eyes were closed. "It would be worse if you weren't here though."

"May that be true in every aspect of my life," Fain said, letting Fir go. "Your eyes are hazel."

"Yes," Fir replied.

"I don't think I knew that."

"You probably didn't need to."

"With little splinters of green like pine needles."

"How fitting."

"Yes. Anyways. You can have the bed."

"Where are you going to sleep?"

"The chair."

"I won't sleep if I know you're stuck in a chair because of me."

"Well, the bed is pretty small, but we can try to fit side by side."

Over the past several months, Fir had nearly forgotten the reassuring discomfort of sleeping beside someone. Fain disappeared easily into the deep still waters of subconsciousness while Fir lay awake, synchronizing their breath.

GORGEOUS

In the Unwood, the coyote left the pieces of body dense with hair for more desperate scavengers, and gorged on thick wefts of pink muscle rich with the iron tang of blood. Teeth cracked the surfaces of bones and the coyote remembered the sponge of marrow like the slight give of hard earth after rain. The marrow was not needed just then—the coyote would be well-filled by meat that required less work to extract.

Innards leaked outward and human scent scattered through trees and grass, a rare smell in the forest and stronger than it had been there for countless years.

The coyote was not the first to the flesh. Flies are always quicker because they are never gone from any place; they lay their eggs before any mammal notices the new death. Maggots taste of swelling wounds, so the coyote ate around them rather than through them.

As body was devoured, flesh became easier to claw away from bone. The Coyote went slowly, kept the vultures waiting in the sky, watched for rats creeping forward to claim their piece, ready to kill anyone who came too close before their time.

Live bodies taste better than dead ones.

PINEAPPLE

Slip finds it easy to speak to The Corpses, for their silences are cups into which words can be poured. Any words. The dead have no need to drink and, therefore, no reason to prefer one drink over another. Yet talking to them is still more than talking to oneself, for there is always a possibility, however remote, that they might hear.

The first time Slip speaks to The Corpses, the Unwood's forest floor transforms—a magic trick of memory—into the basement floor of the childhood home where Slip once sat on the carpet with a pencil and a notebook, during a party thrown by Slip's parents, talking to a friend of the family who sprawled like a crabapple tree. Even immobile, lying on the couch and drunk on cherry brandy, Crabapple's limbs were too long and gnarled for such a cramped space.

"I hate arithmetic," Slip said in the voice of relatively untroubled youth for whom school is life's single great bane.

"Me too," Crabapple mumbled, half-conscious.

"All these numbers moving about, joining together, splitting apart, getting smaller, getting bigger, never staying still, and for what?" Tender graphite snapped beneath the pressure of Slip's right hand.

"Ridiculous," Crabapple agreed. "Like dead bodies."

"What on earth do you mean?"

"We bury them, they turn to soil, we bury more bodies in the soil. Death in death, death on death, death augmenting death, death borrowing from death…" Crabapple sing-songed. "The whole world is a graveyard."

"Don't be gross," Slip scolded.

Talking to The Corpses is like talking to Crabapple. *Do they hear? Will they remember?* Slip thinks no one can know for certain, but it still feels different than loneliness.

"Hi," Slip says to The Corpses, adjusting the red wool scarf so it makes a complete circle around the bones. "Hello. I feel like maybe I should introduce myself properly? I just started talking at you before without saying anything about myself. Though I confess I don't know what to tell you. I could give you my name, but you would have no use for it. You can't say it or write it down, and I don't think anyone will come here to talk to you about me. You only need to learn the sound of my voice so that when you hear me speak, you will know who is addressing you."

The gathered bones have begun to set in the soil, prim with the artificial order of a staged archaeological dig. Slip is concerned about being outwitted by them, or outmannered; The Corpses know both life and death but Slip has never been dead and so seems to be at an epistemological disadvantage. This new source of worry is a surprise to Slip, for who among us expects to feel a need to withhold information from interlocutors who cannot communicate? *Of course,* Slip thinks, *if The Corpses are truly well-mannered and wise with age and experience, they should not hold their longevity against me.*

"You might want to know why I'm visiting you, especially since it seems that you've been here for a long time without being disturbed by anyone. I used to come often, but before I happened upon you I hadn't been here for a long while. Perhaps you know that age has its limits. My health was rather tenuous in the recent past. Don't trouble yourselves about it, I'm well enough now, and in a phase where I don't have to care all the time about how I'm feeling. I'm sure I'll grow out of it though." Slip snickers.

Rain falls like music notes in the Unwood, the sky a wide piano over the forest clearing. While most of the animal inhabitants have retreated to the cozy interiors of dry trees or the hospitable verandas formed by dense branches, the earthworms, having heard the tiny vibrations of each splashing drop of water, are emerging from dampening soil to begin their slick migrations over ground made newly traversable.

"I used to come here because of the animals. They don't talk to me any more than you do, but they do respond, in their way, when I walk through the forest and that's a kind of comfort. I have none of that old fear of the beast in the human face. In fact, I wish the animal were more obvious in us. Back in civilization, people are numbed by structure. They've lost the vigilance that is a form of respect. They have ears but they don't really listen, they have eyes but they can stare right through you as if you're not even there. Deer never do that. Sometimes they run, sometimes they stay, but they always know where I am.

"There is something creaturely about you dead and I know I'm not the only one to notice it. You're not exactly like the deer, I can't say for sure whether you know where I am, but you're not like living people either because I also can't say for sure that your attention is fixed somewhere else. You might be aware of me, you might not. As long as there's a chance, I don't mind too much."

Dirt has layered itself into the webbed crevices of The Corpses' bones and Slip's sleeve descends on the skeletal fragments one by one to clear the dust away. One of the long bones is bisected by an unusually large groove so deep and wide that it readily admits the tip of a scouring fingernail. Skip wants to know what happened there. Is it gauche to pose questions to people who cannot answer? Slip is not sure and so refrains, time after time, from asking The Corpses anything, while an inner compendium of unarticulated queries increases proportionally. For instance: *Who are you? Why are you in the Unwood? Where were you before you were here? Which of the animals ate from your body? Do you think of your future, and if you do, how do you envision it unfolding?*

"If I were a different kind of person, I suppose I'd report you to the police. That sounds unfriendly. As though I think you shouldn't be here. But I'm happy you're here. I just wonder if you want someone to help you find your family. Maybe not, maybe you're like me. Still, you might like for someone to find your killer, if you were killed. It's strange how intimate murder is, isn't it?" Slip allows rhetorical questions like these. "Blood on the ground, blood in the veins, they bind us the same," Slip recites, touching index finger to lips in a ritualistic gesture. "Of course, for all I know, it was a chance calamity that killed you."

Birds of wilder spaces, being so unused to human company, are generally far more timid than those who inhabit parks and other domesticated foliage. This maxim holds true for most of the feathered lifeforms of the Unwood, who observe Slip from a wary distance. The single gregarious exception to this rule is perched on the antler of a staghorn sumac, a few feet from where Slip and The Corpses are sitting. The starling scintillates among the dark leaves, clutching that bony growth of tree as Slip holds up an equally osseous remnant of human life.

"You might like to know why I'm not going to the police," Slip offers The Corpses considerately. Ordinarily, Slip would give an interlocutor an opportunity to reply, but somehow that seems insulting when one is speaking to those who cannot say anything, like trying to teach a dog to use a fork. "I will say this: the police have taken me to places where I was not safe and told me I was home, and the police have taken me from places where I was safe and told me I was not welcome. I wouldn't want them to make the same mistake with you."

If The Corpses do not look grateful, it is hard to say they do not look satisfied by this answer.

Slip, reluctant to soliloquize for too long without offering the audience reprieve, stands up from the flat rock that has served as a seat. Once again, Slip spirals the clearing looking for unnoticed scraps of clothing or jewelry submerged in muck, and comes up empty-handed. It is possible that scavengers have scattered the remnants of personal identity, but the completeness of the eradication suggests otherwise.

As Slip approaches the threshold of the Unwood, meaning to leave, the starling calls, *Cor, cor!* As if trying to say *corpses.* As if this is not the first time the bird has heard a human speak. Slip turns to the bird, replies, "Cor."

Somehow, a rucksack doesn't seem like the right vessel for the deceased, but there is nothing better, so Slip just tries not to pack away the bones like tent poles. Spoken words fall, snowflakes over mud.

"Other people don't seem to think I'm normal, but I can't see how I'm all that odd. I might be speaking to dead bodies right now—which I grant you maybe lots of people don't do—but I never *expected* to be talking to dead bodies, probably like most people don't expect to talk to dead bodies, and that's normal, right? I'm at most half-abnormal. I bet a lot of people are partly abnormal. They're not robots after all, are they?

"Besides, I'd also bet that there are lots of people who *do* talk to dead bodies. Morticians must. Those doctors who do autopsies, probably. And can you imagine committing murder and not even talking to the body after? Psychics, of course. Look, those are whole categories of people who speak to dead bodies. I'm just part of yet another category of people that is less easy to name but definitely does still talk to dead bodies. One of my grandparents used to tell stories to the ashes of the other, did it all the time and got along fine for years, didn't need anybody's help with daily life—not for that anyways—and eventually died in perfect peace. Maybe that's me then, one of *many* lonely old people who do this. I didn't understand then, of course. Young people never do. If I had known what I know now…no, no, pay it no mind. Someone has to talk to the dead, right?"

Slip swaddles the bones in silk handkerchiefs before laying them one over the other.

"You don't look like you ever got a funeral. Every passage needs a ceremony, though—maybe this is yours. You know, if you wanted to have more say in it, you should have left a note. I hope you like that name, by the way, 'The Corpses.' Your fault, again, if you don't. I thought about it for a long time." And Slip had: carcasses sounded too predatory, cadavers too clinical, dead bodies too casual, victims too presumptuous, bones too reductive, remains too antiquated, vestiges of flesh too unspeakably pompous.

If in possession of a comprehensive dictionary and an interest in etymology, Slip might have known that the word *corpse* comes from the Middle English *corps,* a word which could be used to refer to the body of a human or an animal, whether living or dead. Narrowing of meaning occurred over time. As it is, Slip does not know this genealogy, at least not consciously, though perhaps may sense it, the way branches can feel the pull of other branches moving in the wind, the way trees correspond with each other through scent and slow pulse.

"Oh well, you're beyond any harm I can do you now. A reputation matters so long as we move through the world, wearing it as our face, but there's no good or bad that can come to you from a legacy anymore. You're past being hurt so you must be past resentment, too."

The rucksack does not close easily, begs to spill, but at last concedes to the thin-skinned, slow-blooded, insistent fingers of Slip, who recognizes, with a surge of discouragement upon hoisting the freight, how long the walk back to the park will feel. Foot over foot Slip goes, chanting *Can I take another step before I rest?* Sometimes, the answer is no.

Having, at last, at an hour far later than expected, turned onto the road leading into The Singing Frog, Slip does not stop again, not wanting to draw undue attention to the procession, only slowing once to throw a glance toward the management office, where a dandelion bloom of lamplight brings the outline of the manager—hand on hip, staring absently at an upper corner of the room, nodding along to someone's voice on the telephone—into fuzzy relief. In the section of the park with the largest RVs, Slip overtakes a subdued teenager shuffling along alone, and passes a small party out on a veranda, hearing the bells of ice in their glasses, catching the ragged edges of their rowdy laughter but missing the communal joke.

The table in the trailer is too small and the bed is too intimate, so Slip sets the rucksack down on the couch.

"There," Slip says to The Corpses. "Now you're like company."

Slip sits on the chair at the dinette table, watching the rucksack, which does not move, and yet, as time drips by, its appearance shifts, readjusts, until it looks like an envelope concealing a bomb that has been laid purposely out of place.

"That won't do. You'll never get comfortable."

Slip removes the parcels from the bag, slipping the bones from the canvas of their second flesh.

"I hope you're happy here, or will be. I worry that I'm wrong, that in fact you chose the Unwood with intent, that maybe you truly meant for it to be your final resting place."

A sesamoid nodule tumbles onto the floor.

"Are you trying to get back to it?"

Slip begins to carefully arrange individual bones on the cushions of the couch.

"When I die, it won't matter where they bury me. The only company I expect is beetles."

Rucksack emptied, the bones occupy the length of the couch horizontally and the skull sits upright in the middle of the couch's back.

"There. That's better."

Slip goes to the cabinet, then the fridge, pours pineapple juice over ice cubes in a lowball glass, and raises a toast to The Corpses.

"I can't offer you a drink, but how about some music?"

Static crackles as the dial rolls through AM stations, settling on the emphasized off-beats of a big band swing number.

"I'm not really of the time I'm living in anymore. Neither are you. That's why it makes sense for us to be here together."

POLYONYMOUS

Bodies have at least four names.

I

    At the moment of birth, the living body is given a name. It does not know this name. It does not call itself by this name.

II

    At the moment before death, the living body has a name. It knows this name. It calls itself by this name.

III

    As a living body turns into a dead one, it becomes a different creature altogether. For four minutes after its last breath, the body will not relinquish its form. After that, there is chaos. The parts of the body can no longer agree on anything. Muscles refuse to move while skin loosens its attachment and warmth leaves in waves. Cells eat themselves without meaning to. The brain cries itself to sleep. If the body has language after this, it is a language softening and guttering, losing shape and import—a language no one can read.

Unfamiliar bacteria and insects attend the new body, which swells in size as if to accommodate them. The body takes the colour of aurora blueberries, of purple sea stars, of nautical twilight when the horizon begins to disappear. Nails and teeth are shed. Organs and muscles rush out like meltwater—mass exodus— and the vestiges of the body's shape do not hold.

During its last time as itself, the body will be simplified to bone. The familiar is rendered entirely unrecognizable to those who loved it most. The once living body has become a different creature altogether. This is why, when a body dies, it may need a new name. A name it has never had before.

IV

In the end, even the bones crack open and disintegrate into the world. This is why all bodies share the same final name: *Omnia.*

AUTOSTEREOGRAM

Blue and Culver had been missing for one month and four days when Fir realized that something was wrong, well and truly wrong, with the lovers—that the problem was far more dire than anyone's wounded feelings.

"Where are we searching today?" Fain was standing in the driveway next to the car and fidgeting with the keys.

"We should leave the neighbourhood," Fir said.

"Can you think of anywhere they liked to go?"

"Not really." Fir shrugged, eyes on the ground.

"Hiking trails?"

"Probably they hiked. I wouldn't know where."

"Conservation areas? Abandoned houses?"

"They weren't teenagers looking for somewhere to fuck."

"Well people don't disappear to high-end furniture boutiques. We have to think of where they might have gone and not been seen. Farms? Cemeteries? Even slightly remote places."

"How would I know!"

"Just try to remember anything you can." Though it was only midafternoon, the sky was so overcast that it might have been dusk. The clouds were indistinct, and manifest in the sky as widespread murk. "Do you know where their families are buried?"

"Looks like rain," Fir said, finally looking up.

"It's not going to rain."

"Maybe we should call it off."

"This isn't going to be any easier next time."

"We have nowhere to go anyways."

"Okay, you said they might have been hikers. Let's run with that. I have an idea." Fain unlocked the passenger side door and nudged Fir toward it.

Fain's car was a rusted-out rattletrap sub-compact hatchback whose original paint colour was no longer discernible. It might have once been any of a range of medium-to-dark neutral colours, but that hue had been permanently altered by sunlight and persistent filth, and the car existed now on a continuum between grey, taupe, and mauve depending on the relative brightness of the sky and the length of time for which the car had gone unwashed. The car was a stick-shift and Fain rammed it bodily through its gears. It roared onto the main street, the roaring being less a function of speed and more one of pure dysfunctional noise. Almost immediately they were out of the minuscule downtown—six blocks of low-rise brick buildings from the early twentieth century—and into the quaint penumbra of the suburbs.

"I didn't even know you had a car," Fir said.

"I'm sure you can imagine why I only drive it when I need to."

"Not too many kilometres left in the engine?"

"And it attracts a lot of attention." Fain laid on the gas pedal for emphasis, bringing the growling sounds of the car to a grotesque crescendo.

Within ten minutes, they were past the neighbourhoods and into the rolling hay fields and cattle barns. The day's hazy humidity had become tangible once they reached the country, obscuring the branches of trees and the lines of houses. Fir expected water to fill a cupped hand hanging out the window.

"Where are we going?" Fir asked.

"It's just a forest I know. It has walking paths in it, but they're badly maintained and don't get a lot of traffic. It'd be easy to go unnoticed in there."

"You're not thinking of the Unwood are you?"

"Of course not. The Unwood doesn't have hiking paths."

"Right." Fir had long regarded the town furor over the Unwood as a kind of collective paranoia, but also had no reason to take an interest in the area, and often went months or years without thinking of it at all—then was always rather surprised when reminded of the mythic status that had managed to attach itself to an otherwise humdrum bunch of trees. "So where are we going?"

"It's just this hiking trail on the opposite side of Euphoria. What's it called? Lowhill, I think."

"I think I know the one you mean."

"Anyways, like I said, it'd be easy to go unnoticed in there, if you got lost or something."

"I have trouble imagining it being a trail so long that you're likely to get lost on it."

"Well, yes, not…exactly…but anything's possible."

"Do you think they're dead?"

"Do you?"

"Please just tell me."

"I think maybe they simply up and left. And don't want anyone to know."

Fir considered that for a moment.

"I think I'd rather they were dead," Fir said. "Is that terrible?"

"Well…" Fain began, buying time. After a weighted interval: "Why would you rather they were dead?"

"Because if they're not dead then we really meant nothing to each other."

"Well…"

"It's an awful way to think. I know it is."

"Not *awful*…"

"Monstrously selfish."

"No, I get why you'd feel that way. I don't know if I would in your place, but I can see how it would come to that."

Fir moaned, a lonely orca.

"Maybe they're being held hostage," Fain offered. Fir made no reply, so Fain forged ahead. "It's better to keep thinking they're alive. Dead bodies are harder to find. Half the time, when they are found, it's because some stranger wandering in the middle of nowhere stumbled over them."

Privately, Fir thought that such buoyant optimism could only be sustained by standing at a distance from the problem and making friends with contradiction—Fir was unable to feel either so alienated or so amiable. "How well do you think the police searched their house, if they did at all?" Fir asked. "I mean, if they are dead, their bodies could be well-hidden. Maybe the police just went in, checked that no living people were walking around and no notes were sitting on the kitchen table and left?"

"It's possible, I guess. Death tends to have a smell though."

"What if the bodies were buried in the basement and the hole was filled over with concrete?"

"Yeah, in that case probably there wouldn't be much of a smell."

"Do you think we should check the house ourselves?"

"We can put it on the list of things to do."

"How will we get in?"

"We'll probably have to break in. I can't imagine that they'll try too hard to prosecute, if anyone even notices we're there."

"It's not a cheap house though. Could have an alarm system."

"Yeah, but if an alarm goes off we can just leave."

"What if it's a silent alarm?"

"Do you want me to go by myself?" Fain said it without anger, as if offering to go alone to pick up a prescription from the pharmacy.

"No, of course I'd go with you. I just want to make sure we know what we're getting into. That we're not in over our heads."

"We've been in over our heads since this started. No reason to stop now." The car slowed and pulled to a stop on the road's wide gravel shoulder. "Hey. We're here."

The countryside seemed eerily quiet after the cacophony of the engine. Casting eyes ahead and behind, Fir noted a stretch of grass by the roadside and woods beyond that, but could discern nothing remarkable about either of them. "Where are we?"

"There's a trail."

"I don't see a trail."

"Get out of the car, I'll show you," Fain said, stepping out. "And don't forget to lock your door."

"Right." Fir pressed down the manual lock and slammed the door shut, before following Fain to a gap in the woods indicated by a small, faded wooden sign that hadn't been visible from the road.

Foliage, though trampled-down, evenly covered the path they walked.

"I have difficulty believing that this is a real trail," Fir said.

"You're not dreaming," Fain replied.

They traipsed slowly, scanning the forest floor with unfocused eyes, as if trying to find the hidden image in an autostereogram.

"You've been here before," Fir remarked. "Do you see anything that looks different?"

"I haven't been in years. I had an ex who used to bring me here for the…seclusion," Fain said delicately.

"Oh!" Fir replied, turning away to conceal a flush. "That's lucky." A pause. "I mean lucky for us that because of your ex we have somewhere to look. It's useful to know about out of the way places when looking for missing people. Very fortunate indeed." Fir braved a swift glance at Fain—who was suppressing a smirk—and felt an ache for something lost, or repressed, or forgotten, but could not say precisely what.

Fir had resolved not to speak again until spoken to but, after 15 minutes of uninterrupted greenery, felt compelled to adorn the silence. "See anything? Anything worth mentioning?" It was a useless question; Fir knew that. Asked as if Fain had reason to conceal some poignant observation.

"Well, I did notice some poison ivy, so watch out?"

After that Fir could see nothing in the forest but trinities of leaves.

"This is maddening," Fir said, when Fain stopped to toe over something gleaming on the ground that turned out to be a bottle cap. "The woods are so dense I can't see more than a few feet past the sides of the path. There could be a body—a person—six feet away from us and we'd never even realize."

"Yeah."

"How long is this trail?"

"Not all that far really. We're almost halfway through. Soon it will curve back around and come out about half a kilometre from where the car is parked. But we're getting close to a clearing.

That's where people, you know, hang out. So we can spend some extra time combing that area especially thoroughly."

They walked on, mosquito trill filling their ears and mayflies clouding their eyes.

"This trail looks like hardly anyone's used it lately," Fir observed.

"That's how it always looks. Okay, I think we're close to the entrance to the clearing now. Keep an eye out. It'll be on our right-hand side."

Their already small steps turned to mincing for a few hundred metres as they scoured for portals in the foliage, but they could see none large enough to admit a person.

"Does it still exist? I thought we'd have passed it by now," Fain said. "Let's double back."

They nearly returned to the point at which they had started looking for the clearing. "I don't get it," Fain sighed. "I—oh! Wait, wait, wait. This might be it. But it's very overgrown. Just stay here for a minute." Fain crouched down and scuttled away into the underbrush.

Fir stood alone on the path, watching the spot that Fain had disappeared into. The sound of rustling branches became increasingly faint, then it too vanished.

"Everything all right?" Fir called. The rustling resumed, grew, until Fain popped back onto the path with scratched cheeks.

"I found it. Come with me."

Fir followed, not convinced that Fain had found anything, feeling that they were only brushing through the narrow gaps between saplings.

"We're here," Fain announced, standing up as the woods opened suddenly into the sky. The clearing was full of tall grass and thistles, and far larger than Fir had expected, more the size of an amphitheatre than a mere break in the trees.

"This grass will take a long time to comb through," Fir noted. "Should we split up?"

"Let's not. If we stay together we'll have two sets of eyes on every square inch and we'll be less likely to miss something."

"Right."

They walked, single-file, spiralling inward from the perimeter of the clearing, with Fain leading the way as had become their tacit pattern. Fir tripped on a rabbit burrow; Fain trod on a bird carcass.

"Does this look like something either of them would wear?" Fain held up a ratty fleece vest.

"Absolutely not."

Then they found the bone.

They had walked right past it, scarcely visible in the tall grass, but Fir had gone back to check a faint flash of grimy off-white.

"Hey," was all Fir could manage.

"Find something?" Fain turned to look.

Fir held aside the stems of grass, estimated the bone to be a foot in length. "Could this be from a human leg?" Fir asked. "Should we touch it?"

"Use my jacket to pick it up so you don't get your fingerprints on the potential evidence." Fain handed Fir a windbreaker.

"Is it human?" Fir repeated, cradling the bone in nylon.

"I wouldn't know," Fain said. "Could be. Or it could be from a large animal."

"Where's the rest of the skeleton?"

"Let's keep looking and see if we can find it."

"Should we call the police?"

"You can try."

Fir had to redial the number three times with trembling hands.

"Yes, hello? I need to report that I have found a bone. I think it might be human."

Fir stared up at the sky and answered a series of infuriatingly mundane questions before being allowed to tell the story of the bone.

"I found—I mean my friend and I found—a bone on a hiking trail—actually I'm not sure it's an official hiking trail—but it's some kind of path that obviously lots of people go on that's right off Highway Four—yes today—just now in fact—well of course it's suspicious I mean it looks like a human leg bone and it's in the middle of the woods. No, I haven't seen a lot of human leg bones, I'm not a doctor, but I get the gist of what they look like and we were out here in the first place looking for two friends of ours who are missing, so what if it's one of their leg bones? No they wouldn't be in your database. They're not officially missing—of course I tried to make a report but the officer decided I wasn't close enough to them to know whether they were actually missing or not but that doesn't mean they aren't missing you know and don't you think it's strange that we went looking for them and found this bone? Don't you think you should at least—you know what, never mind." Fir ended the call.

"That doesn't sound like it went well."

"We're just going to bring the bone into the station ourselves. What are they going to do, turn us out of the station in front of a bunch of civilians when we look like we've uncovered a murder? No, then they'll listen to us, I'm sure of it."

"Are we going to finish searching the area first?"

"Right, yes, yes we are, how could I forget that."

"A lot has happened. It's normal to lose track."

"Yes a lot has happened. That's right."

"How about you just hold onto that bone and follow me?"

"You got it. I mean I got it. You know what I mean."

Fir was giddy with anticipation and agonism. The clearing around them refused to be still, circling them as they circled it, predators staring each other down.

"I guess if this turns out to be anything, the police will do their own search of the area," Fir said, trying to believe it was true, for Fir was finding it difficult to concentrate on anything but the bone they had already found. If Fir did not think continuously of the bone, it might cease to exist, being as it was nearly weightless in the hand, like a flimsy accident of no consequence at all.

"You can't trust other people to be perfect," Fain chided. "We might as well finish our work and walk the last half of the trail as we planned. No sense in being careless."

"You're right, you're right," Fir conceded reluctantly, despite wanting to go to the station immediately to narrow the interval between first discovery and final epiphany.

"Are you doing okay?" That question had become part of their routine debriefing, habitually initiated by Fain, who was asking it again as they emerged from the trail and began following the road back to the car. The roadside ditch was overgrown with day lilies, bright as clementines, and Fir thought that this might not be the worst place to die.

"Yeah, definitely," Fir replied. "I'm very okay."

The exhaustion of aftermath had settled over Fir and the half-kilometre back to the car felt unbearably long. Left foot forward. *The bone belongs to someone I know.*

Right foot forward. *The bone belongs to no one I know.* Fate could be reduced to a pattern of feet on stone and that was reason enough to go on.

"Which is better?" Fir brooded. "The grief of death or the ambiguity of indefinite loss?"

"What's worse is going back and forth from one to the other like you have been for months. At least, regardless of what we learn, identifying this bone will bring you a little closer to the truth." Was there a measure of tried patience in Fain's voice? It had been an unusually tense day for them. "Where is the police station anyways? I don't think I've ever been there."

"Not even for work?" Fir inquired.

"No. We call them if there's a problem and they come to us. And honestly, I've never been involved in any serious problems. The most I've had to do is give a brief statement at the scene. Never needed to go in and file a report or anything like that."

"That's probably a good thing." Fir stood by the car waiting for Fain to unlock the manual door. "I'll direct you."

"When were you there?" Fain asked. There was a beat of silence. "Sorry, you don't have to answer that if you don't want to."

"Turn left here, then right at the corner," Fir said as Fain pulled out. "Don't worry. It's nothing dramatic. One of my parents was just a drunk and not very good at hiding it."

"Sometimes I forget that you grew up in Euphoria."

"And you can't figure out why I stayed? Trust me, what's stranger by far is that you moved here voluntarily."

"Well, I didn't fall in love with the town, I fell in love with someone here. Anyways, I grew up an hour down the road, where my parents still live, so close I can visit them weekly. It wasn't much of a stretch."

"Turn right onto the next street. How'd you meet your ex?"

"Oh, you know," Fain said. "How does anyone meet anyone?" Every time Fain spoke about the past, it became a wider chasm.

"Why'd you stay?"

"I figured if I can't be happy in Euphoria, where can I ever hope to be happy?" Fain laughed. "What about you? How come you never left? You don't seem to be in love with the town either."

"It does not elate me, no. Turn left at the next stop sign."

"The one that's like five minutes down the road?"

"Yeah. I'm here because of the usual reasons that people stay in their hometowns. I didn't have anywhere else I wanted to go. It was easy to stay here, get a job, keep close to my parents and siblings." *And Blue?* Fir could not say that out loud. It sounded ridiculous, even if it was true. Fain, of course, would receive such a proclamation with nonchalant serenity, but Fir needed it to remain ineffable— a possible explanation, rather than a declarable reality. "Geographically close, anyways. I can't say we have a deep emotional connection. But tell me Fain, am I missing out? Is the rest of the world terrifically exciting?"

"I wouldn't know," Fain said. "I've only seen so much of it. I have this theory that small towns are like really dense planets. Despite their size, they have a gravity about them. It's hard to take yourself completely out of their orbit."

"That sounds about right." Fir sighed and gestured the next direction. "That way. What I don't understand is how anyone gets lost in Euphoria. I mean, how much of this town is untrodden land? None of it. There's nowhere new to go in this nowhere town." A bitterness was rising in Fir's throat that Fain seemed to sense.

"There might not be any new places under the sun," Fain said. "But there are always places that haven't seen daylight for years."

"Go straight through the roundabout. I just feel like we're running out of places to look. Like what will we do if this bone turns out to be nothing? Euphoria's too small and the rest of the world is too much. But if I'm not looking for them, then who is? I've got to go on. I guess I just have to keep circling farther out forever until I find them or I die."

"A widening gyre. Let's not get ahead of ourselves though. We still have the house, one of the most important possible places."

"I should remind you again that you're a good friend."

"And I should remind you again that, though I regret the grim circumstance, this is the most exciting thing that's likely to happen all year."

"See that sign? Turn into the parking lot and we're here."

They sat in the parked car at first, not taking off their seat belts.

"Do you want me to come with you?" Fain finally asked.

"Yeah. It'll make me look less like a lone conspiracy theorist."

"It's only a true conspiracy if you have followers."

The police station was a squat, single-storey brick building that looked as bland as any set of white-collar offices, hardly the formidable and imposing fortress one might expect.

Inside, Fain concealed the bone while Fir told a disengaged receptionist that they had possibly found a dead body and wanted to speak with an officer.

"Possibly?" The receptionist arched an eyebrow.

Fir and Fain waited on undersized chairs with fake leather seats while people who arrived after them were seen before them.

"I guess we're low priority." Fir said. "Do they not believe that we found a dead body? I don't even want to give a statement. I just want to drop this off and have them call me once they've figured out who it belongs to."

TOOTHBRUSH

In the library, Slip retrieves books on taxidermy and trophy hunting and studies them for chapters devoted to the cleaning of bones. With horror, Slip reads that hot water will shrink them and peroxide will bleach them. This is not at all what Slip had in mind— the objective is to bathe them, not to change them to a new form. Fear sprawls, and in the end, Slip is immobile, holding a bone over a bowl of cold water, tilting a toothbrush toward it, unable to be reconciled even to this minor intervention. The dust on the bones of The Corpses, like their colour and their size, must remain the same.

PROBABLE DEAD BODY

"So you think you found a dead body," the police officer said, looking up from the intake form. "But you're not sure?"

"A dead *human* body. We found a piece," Fir explained, as Fain double-checked that the door to the office was closed, and delicately unfolded the windbreaker to reveal the bone. The officer glanced at the bone, then stared at Fir and Fain incredulously. Fir pressed on. "This almost certainly—I think, correct me if I'm wrong— must belong to a dead body."

"And I see," the officer glanced at the intake form again, "that you found this in the woods of Lowhill off Highway Four. Where, I assume, dwell any number of large non-human animals to whom this bone might belong."

"But we were there looking for our two missing friends and we have *reason to believe* that this might belong to them," Fir insisted.

"Ah! Missing persons." The officer swivelled briskly to face a computer.

"Not officially missing," Fir corrected sheepishly. "I did report, a little over a month ago."

"And?" The officer cocked a suspicious eye at Fir.

"They'd only been missing for a few days at the time. The officers didn't think there was sufficient reason to be concerned, so they didn't open an investigation, at least not based on my report."

"Did you ever talk to the family or social circle of your missing friends?"

"I'd only ever met the one set of parents, and I did reach out, but they said they hadn't heard from my friend for a while, which makes sense, because they had kind of a strained relationship."

"Uh-huh. How about you give me your friends' names and I'll see what I can find out. Maybe someone else reported them missing after you did."

Fir spelled out Blue and Culver's full names, and gave the officer their address.

"Very curious," the officer said, slowly pivoting away from the computer and back toward Fir and Fain. "I don't see any open investigations. How could people be missing for three months, but not reported as such by anyone except you, do you suppose?"

Fir shrugged. "Like I said, they had pretty distant relationships with their families. And I'm sure they had friends, but none they dutifully checked in with, as far as I know. They were self-employed, did a lot of contract work, probably more likely to be sued by their business connections if they disappeared than to be reported missing."

The officer coughed. "People don't just vanish without arousing suspicion."

"No," said Fir, "but they can gradually fade out of people's lives without being missed too much. I think that they were— going through a lot in the months leading up to their disappearance. They withdrew from a lot of people."

"Except you."

"Oh, they withdrew from me, too. I guess I was just bothered by it more than others in their lives."

The officer's eyes were narrowed, thin as paper cuts. Fir was suddenly less afraid of being disbelieved and more afraid of being seen as a person of interest in a yet-to-be-determined crime.

"How about you tell me what reason you have to believe that this bone belongs to the not-officially-missing persons in question?" the officer said finally.

"It's a bone we found while looking for our *suspected* missing friends in a place we *suspected* them to be." The expression was patently clumsy. Outwardly, Fir reddened and inwardly, Fir self-castigated. Fain offered a consoling hand on the shoulder.

"And why did you *suspect* them to be there?"

"It was a place they loved to hike." Fain intervened. "They told Fir about it. On numerous occasions. Kept saying we should go sometime ourselves. It's a secluded place though. Somewhere a person might fall and no one would find them. That kind of thing. It made sense to check for them there after not seeing them for a while." Fir sat rigidly, grateful for, and terrified of, Fain's simplifying lie.

"Uh-huh." The officer appeared to be considering what to say next.

"You know," Fain plowed on. "There are some people in Euphoria who say that small-town police are useless. Just giving out parking tickets to people who exceeded their meter by a few minutes. I always tell them it's not true. That, sure, maybe that's what the police do day-to-day, but when it really counts, the police still stand up and step in to keep us safe."

"Err, yes." The officer coughed. "Ahem. Thank you—for that. But it's not up to me whether possible *evidence* is sent out for forensic testing. My superiors will make that call. So I will bring this to them and see what they say."

"And then you'll be in touch?" Fain asked.

"Someone will be in touch with you if there's any further communication required."

"If you identify the bone, you'll let us know?" Fain pressed.

"We will let you know if there's any further communication required."

"That's not a yes."

"Look." The officer's hands were flattened on the top of the desk. "What I expect we will find is that this is a deer bone. In which case there will be no reason for us to have further contact."

"Wait a minute," Fir said. "A *deer* bone? How would you know that?"

"I'm a hunter," the officer replied.

"Of course you are," Fain muttered, standing up. "Well, this has been extremely helpful." Fain gently nudged Fir, who rose shakily. "Thank you so much for your time. We truly look forward to speaking with you again when—"

"*If*—"

"*When* the occasion arises," Fain said, ushering Fir out of the door.

TWITCH

Tires skid, handlebars shake, and the kids' bikes come to shrill and abrupt stops.

"Fucking quitch," Mal shouts, spitting out an electric green hard candy and flinging it at the back of the car that missed them by inches and is now peeling away into the night. The wet gob of sugar sticks to the trunk of the car with a diminutive *thunk* that goes unnoticed by the driver. Both kids shift the weight off of their left legs and start pedalling again.

"Anyways, like I was saying," Mal continues, "I think we should go to that party tonight. It's not that far of a ride and we can leave if there's nothing interesting going on."

"I thought we were going back to my house to watch movies. I mean, why'd we get movies if that's not what we're doing?"

"We can do that after we get back from the party. It's, what, like eight? It's barely dark yet."

"We don't even hang out with anyone who'll be there."

"Speak for yourself. Besides, how do we know who'll show up? Maybe you'll meet someone you like for once."

"I like…" *You,* Limn thinks.

"Who?" Mal asks.

"People. There are lots of people I like."

"I don't even know if you like me and I'm the only person you ever spend time with who's not a blood relative."

"I do like your company," Limn says, hesitant, careful not to sound too earnest, or ardent.

"Okay. That's cool. I mean, glad we got that established, 'cause if you like me you might be capable of liking other people, too. Come on, go to the party with me, it'll be good for you."

"Nah, you go. Stop by my place after, though. My parent's out. We can watch one of our movies."

"And what are you going to do with yourself all night?"

"It's a big secret. I'll tell you when I see you later."

"Yeah right. Probably going to read one of your novels, or paint with watercolours or something, because you're a ten-thousand-year-old weirdo in a teenager's body."

"Shut up," Limn says, shoulders hunching, knees angling inward.

The kids don't talk again until they're out in the suburbs.

"I'm turning here," Mal announces, slowing as they approach a corner that leads to a residential street Limn has never travelled on purpose.

"Hanging out with the bougie kids tonight, huh?" Limn says disdainfully.

"Enjoy your book and your tea and I'll see you later."

"I don't drink tea!" Limn shouts at Mal's dwindling silhouette.

THE PEOPLE THEY WERE CLOSEST TO

It had been 20 days since Fir had last seen Blue or Culver.

"What's that?" Fain asked, gesturing at a small dark mass in the gutter. *A dead bat,* Fir was prepared to say, but as they drew closer, it became obvious that they were looking at a more manufactured relic of death.

"I'll get it," Fain said, picking the item up with a kerchief. The black leather wallet was empty, not so much as a to-do list left inside. "Do you think it belonged to either of them?" Fain asked.

A diner. A right hand. A 20 dollar bill. Fir could picture each of them clearly. This was not the wallet that accompanied them.

"It definitely didn't belong to Blue. Even if it belonged to Culver, what would that tell us?"

"*Us?* Probably nothing."

"Should we take it along?" Fir asked. Fain nodded and wrapped the wallet in the kerchief, depositing it into a messenger bag.

They crisscrossed the wallet's immediate vicinity in grid lines, scrutinizing that area closely, but saw nothing further of note and so resumed their forward trudge.

"If you had to guess, what would you say the chances are of either of us living in a house this big someday?" Fain asked, gesturing vaguely toward the unnecessarily large, single-family homes that populated the quiet, treed street. There were no sidewalks—lawns sloped smoothly and ended abruptly at the asphalt in crisp lines that looked more architectural than horticultural—so Fir and Fain walked slowly and methodically along the roadside.

"23 percent," Fir answered.

"Really? That high?"

"Yeah, well, you're very bright."

"I haven't made much use of it so far."

"You have, just not for your own benefit. You're too interested in other people."

"Hmm. Interested in other people. That's not the same as being nice, is it?"

"Sometimes it is."

"You know, if you want me to be of any help to you, you're going to have to tell me more about these people. Otherwise, how will I know what to look for?"

Fir did not know what to say, having never said much of anything upon this subject to anyone before, apart from what Fain had already heard.

"I'm not sure what else to tell you. So many of the details are… well, they sound generic out of context, don't they? I could tell you what hobbies they have, or what kind of food they eat, and that wouldn't help you pick them out of a crowd. Here's what they look like." Fir's phone displayed a photo of two people, arms around each other's waists, smiling the way people smile when they know they're being looked at. An expression that conveys almost nothing beyond the fact that the individuals had retained at least a scant awareness of, and concern for, social mores, as of the time the photo was taken.

"Great. Well, that will help if they're just wandering about in a crowd I suppose."

"What do you want to know?"

"Were they happy together? Did they ever talk about moving away? How long had they been married?"

"They were neither happy nor unhappy, as far as I can tell. I have not specifically been told that they intended to move away. About 20 years."

"Did they have enemies?"

"Enemies?"

"People they were in conflict with. Did they have *antagonisms?"*

"Yeah, with each other. Like all couples."

"I don't think all couples…"

"You know what I mean. They never got rough with each other or anything, at least so far as I was told. And no, I don't think they were suing their neighbours, or having a multigenerational family feud. They were estranged from their parents, though that was hardly anything dramatic. I don't even think they had affairs. Except the one…"

"That's obviously not it," Fain said. "You said the problems predated the affair."

"That's how it sounded to me."

"Normal people are so hard to figure out."

"What do you mean?"

"Like, if one of them had an obvious vice, that could give us a lead. If one of them was a drug dealer, we could look into who got the bad end of a bargain. But when things happen to so-called respectable people, you're just left wondering what could have possibly gone wrong. They did everything right, so what gives, you know?"

"Yeah, I guess that's it."

The houses of the neighbourhood had cloaked themselves in wide yards, high fences, swaths of willow and ivy.

"It feels like everyone here is trying to live their lives in secret," Fir said, registering how the curtains on the windows were drawn, the lights in unused rooms were turned off, the cars were stowed away in garages, the children's toys were removed from the grass.

"There is no greater privacy than money," Fain replied.

"You'd think it'd be obvious when anything is out of place here, but I suspect that, if anything were, someone would just immediately come and tidy it up."

"You mean someone would pay someone else to tidy it up."

"Ha. I guess."

The streets were so peaceful that Fir and Fain hardly even had to move aside for passing cars.

"Do you think we should be more, uh, proactive?" Fain asked when they had exhausted the first few streets without seeing anything even potentially noteworthy.

"How?"

"Maybe we should ask people if they've seen them."

"Who? We're the only ones out here."

"We can go door to door."

Fir struggled to predict how the people in this area would respond to two scruffy strangers asking after their neighbours, but also had no better suggestion, so shrugged.

"Sure, okay."

Fain stopped in front of the nearest house. "Might as well get started?"

"Might as well," Fir said, despite the considerable reservations that might be raised regarding the imposing facade of the towering red brick house, which confronted them with its complex roof and its windows arched like disdainful eyebrows.

"I'll talk," Fain assured. "Just get ready to show that photo."

Fain rang the doorbell while Fir surveyed the wraparound porch, which was devoid of chairs. A full two minutes after the bell had been rung, someone finally opened the door.

"Can I help you?" asked the stooped figure, holding a silver-tipped and ornately carved cane of solid wood that looked like it cost more than Fain's car. A pair of large glasses were tucked into a front shirt pocket.

"I hope so!" Fain said spiritedly. "We're looking for friends of ours, have you seen them?" Fir felt a nudge in the ribs and produced the photo.

"No," the stooped figure in the doorway answered after barely glancing at the photo without bothering to retrieve glasses from the pocket that held them.

"Do you know these people at all?" Fain pressed.

"No."

"Are you sure? They live so close to you."

The stooped figure glanced up and down the street.

"Where?"

"Around the block. 11 Cream Court," Fain said.

The stooped figure did not reply, but stared expectantly at Fir and Fain, who were unsure of what it was they were failing to do.

"Well, thank you," Fain said.

"Good day," Fir added affectedly.

The stooped figure did not close the door until Fir and Fain had passed the perimeter of the property.

"I wonder what style of house that was," Fain said.

"Gothic revival."

"I would not have expected you to know that."

90

"Blue was an architect," Fir admitted bashfully. "I guess I picked up a few terms."

"Well, if the 23 percent chance future comes to pass, I'm getting one just like it."

Fir wondered whether it was because they were canvassing the houses in midafternoon, or for some more disdainful reason, that few residents answered their doors. A handful did: other presumed retirees, a smattering of harried lone parents, a completely insouciant 20-something whom Fir envied but did not understand.

The only person who would even admit to recognizing the couple in the photo was one of their immediate neighbours, a 30-something on the way out the door in a suit, who, when asked whether the couple had been around lately, paused to consider, and said no, but could not say how long they had been gone, and who, when prompted, opined that perhaps they were off on holiday.

"Leaving all their mail accumulating and their house untended for weeks on end?" Fir asked and was met with an uncomprehending look.

"Why not?" the 30-something neighbour said, and Fir and Fain could think of no brief response, so only said thank you and promptly departed.

The next-door neighbour on the other side, who lived in a large white stucco house and had to be at least twice the age of the neighbour they had just spoken with, only offered a fed-up *harrumph* when Fir held up the photograph, then promptly shut the door in Fir and Fain's faces.

"Do they really not recognize the people they share a street with?" Fain asked when they were back on a sidewalk.

"Or are they all hiding something?"

"I have no idea." Fir tried to recall the faces of neighbours, but could only summon blurry features and indistinct hair colours. "Honestly I probably couldn't pick some of my neighbours out of a lineup either."

"What kind of flowers are those?" Fain pointed to a profusion of blooms with yellow crêpe petals and long spindling leaves that bookended a driveway they were passing.

"You're really fixated on names today," Fir said evasively. The flowers were jonquils.

"I just want to know what things are."

"What good is a name? It won't tell you when the flowers will blossom or where they want to live or whether they're poisonous or what they are vulnerable to or where they were raised or what they mean—"

"If I knew their names it would help me find out the rest."

"Maybe it would and maybe you'd do everything you could to try to find out all about them and give them what they needed to survive and they could still die on you and you wouldn't even know why."

"I get it. Living organisms are very unpredictable."

"Why are we even talking about this?" Fir asked. "We're supposed to be gathering information. About people."

"We don't know what we're looking for. It might be helpful just to notice things."

FATHOMS

If the human mind were a place, it would be a body of water, immeasurably deep, where fish, aquatic plants, and microorganisms multiply too quickly to be tracked. Many are consumed as soon as they are born, others persist for years. Of those who endure, some are bright and gaudy and splendid and show themselves off to the glittering sunlight. They are impossible to miss. Others—who can say what they look like—hide away in the remoteness of shadows, seen rarely if at all by other creatures. At the very bottom of the water is rock, older than everything but the water itself. And the rock, slowly atomizing into silt and sand, is dusted with the remains of decaying life forms, like a forest floor covered with shed fur and fallen leaves.

Memories, slippery and silver-scaled, swim in schools, fins of a kind that find one another, over and over again. It has been said that no fish ever leave the water, but only get lost in the immensity of that wet, caliginous night. For those fish who are lost, there are scant relics by which to remember them. Sometimes all that remains is a rumour of lurking teeth, or a swimmer's fluttering sense that there are more eyes beneath the water than can ever be counted.

People all over the world feel the loss of the fish in the vast lakes of their thought every day. They sense that they are forgetting something. They may realize that what they are forgetting is both more and less significant than neglecting to get bread at the grocery store, or struggling to recall the order of operations in mathematics, or wondering when one said a childhood classmate's name for the last time. Still, they can't even articulate the species of fish they have forgotten.

When people's feeling of loss is at its most powerful, their fear whispers to them that what they have forgotten is a great secret from their past—their personal past perhaps, or worse, a collective past. They worry that this secret could bite them, take pieces of their body that will never regrow, leave scars for anyone to see. They fret that this secret might be too large, too heavy, that when it weighs upon their backs it will shatter the glossy seashells of their delicate contentment. They dread discovering a secret so awful that the people who hear it will only be able to recoil from one another's bodies in shame, and regard each other with fear and disgust ever after. A secret that, if it ever finds its way to the surface of consciousness, could be driven down but would only keep returning.

Yes, probably all of us have had a displaced feeling of forgetting now and again—as we must. The seemingly infinite details of every waking moment have to blur into the broad shapes of history. For the residents of Euphoria, though, the gnawing, or stinging, or choking awareness that they have forgotten something recurs at least once a day, sometimes more often. In Euphoria—a town that the winds of progress always take longer to reach—time is languid, and the residents are caught in the lag of its waves. They who jet more slowly toward their future are nearer to their past, and their memories trail close behind in their wake. This feeling of forgetting would concern the people of Euphoria, if it were more rare. This forgetting would worry them, if it even once led to remembering.

DIVE

Fir said yes immediately, flushed in the glow of flashbacks to dive bars of decades past: in scant clothes, in the sparse illumination of neon signs and dim amber light, in the high heat of a crowded room and shots of honey bourbon, in the taut clutch of lust. Spells of time they had forgotten how to cast. *Do you need a ride?* Asked as if nothing had changed. *Yes,* Fir said, glad for once not to have a car. Fir always said yes.

PASSENGER SEAT

The nearness of the driver's seat and the passenger seat was overwhelming. Fir gazed out the window, pulse fluttering, as Blue sped toward a town down the road from Euphoria.

ATOMIC SPACING

Fir and Blue did not go to one of their old dive bars, just a diner that served drinks at all hours. Sunlight was shoving its way into their weekday and Fir kept trying to remember what it was they used to talk about for hours.

"What else," Fir said, "is a person supposed to ask a friend—" here Blue's eyes flickered "—they haven't seen in so long?" The question terminated in a short, nervous laugh. "How are your parents? Still alive?"

"Ostensibly."

"Your relationship hasn't improved at all, I take it."

"I don't even visit them on holidays anymore."

"Rough."

"Better than the alternative, though, which would have required me to visit them."

"You'd think they'd get to an age where they'd just…"

"Apologize?"

"Yeah. At least."

"They still think they did nothing wrong. In their minds, it's perfectly acceptable to emotionally cut off their only child for having a *nervous breakdown*—their words of course, not mine—quitting a high-pressure job I only sort of liked, and going to work at a video store."

"You eventually went back to being an architect though."

"Sure, eventually, on a freelance consulting basis. By their standards, I might as well be unemployed. Besides, that only happened after they'd given up on me."

"And you married someone who came from money. That must have pleased them."

"Oh, it did. Isn't that silly? Marriage is just this ceremony that probably had some use in the past but that none of us can now recall. Like a spleen. But we go through the rituals of a wedding anyhow, pretending they are of solemn importance."

"I think it's sort of a nice tradition," Fir said. "A public declaration of love."

"You're so provincial sometimes. Marriage is, more and more, this folksy little festival straight out of a backwater town from the good old days."

"Like Euphoria. Where we live."

"Sure, like Euphoria. Marriage still has a real stranglehold here."

"Stronghold?" Fir asked, but Blue waved it off.

"Hardly anyone in the bigger cities gets married now, except for conservative types. I suppose people are more progressive in the urban centres."

"That's a vast generalization."

"Well, it's true. Look at the way smaller towns vote."

"Euphoria bucks that trend."

"That's why I condescend to live there," Blue said affectedly.

Blue had always possessed a mellow glow of haughtiness. Mild, perhaps, because Blue's contempt was without much conviction.

It might have even been an entirely ironic air. Yet despite regarding all real theatre as a kind of tedious vaudeville, Blue did read through the dramatic lines of everyday life with fervour. And Fir watched, charmed, ready to rush the stage.

"My parents," Blue continued, "obviously agree with you about the merits of marriage. Once I had at least half my job back and the new spouse, they saw fit to have us over for seasonal family dinners again." Blue's voice and eyes dropped, seeming to study the unused cutlery wrapped in paper napkins on the table. "Not more than that. And they wouldn't even deign to call, they'd just send us invitations by mail. The way you'd invite a distant cousin to a funeral."

"Well, at least you saw them that much."

"We did, until we stopped." Blue picked up a butter knife and was excising bits of cork from a coaster. "Back when we did visit, I kept expecting them to bring it up, just once. Even if they didn't say sorry, at least they might mention the fact that they missed the last years of my twenties and the first half of my thirties. But they never did. It was as if that span of my life never occurred. The pretense of it was just too much. And it was so simple to toss the invitations out with the recycling."

"Didn't they call and ask after you?"

"They did. Some half-hearted, *We didn't see you on Sunday. Were you very busy then?* Not the faintest inkling of why I might resent them."

"I'm sorry."

"I was always jealous of how close you were with your parents." Blue looked up, finally, from the tabletop.

"Close," Fir said. "You mean I see them occasionally?"

Blue laughed. "How are they doing?"

"Retired. Both bored and utterly content with their lives."

"Enviable."

"It really is."

"You haven't settled down yet, then?"

"I'm not sure I was ever unsettled. How could I be, living in the same place my whole life?"

"Someone should unsettle you," Blue said. "At least once."

Fir surveyed Blue's face for some hint of how to interpret that sentiment, but found an indecipherable expression there.

"No significant other, then?" Blue continued lightly.

"Well," Fir said. "I'm not married."

A second round of drinks arrived, almost unnoticed; the person who deposited them would have been unrecognizable afterwards, being so little observed.

"Well, okay, we've talked about parents, and our spouses or lack thereof," Fir said. "I think I'm required to ask about kids next. Do you have them? Do you want them?"

"Sure, let's take this from bad to worse."

"I didn't—you don't—"

"No, it's fine. You might as well know. We almost had a child. We had a fetus, for about seven months, and that was the closest we got."

"I'm so—"

"We were sitting together in a hospital room. The doctor came in and said, *You've lost the baby.* And I thought, *That's absurd. That's so impossibly absurd. How can you lose something that's inside of you?*"

Fir touched Blue's hand instinctively and would have drawn back if the grasp were not so quickly returned. There was a timeless and tireless calm just then. After the showing of wounds, neither of them flinched. They turned toward one another instead of away. A surety of being prevailed between them, which Fir suddenly recognized as the transcendence that their years of ephemeral pleasures had tried to imitate.

"I'm so sorry," Fir said.

"That's why we've been working less lately. Backed off most— or in Culver's case, all—of our current projects. Our clients seemed to understand, and we gave them good referrals."

"Of course. Anyone could see that you both need space to be together to face the loss."

"We mourned together at first. Something changed in Culver, though."

"Something like what?"

"Hard to say. I suppose Culver seems ready to give up on life altogether, and I'm not. Worse, it's as if Culver wants me to be equally hopeless, as though commiseration is the only way to get through this. That sounds to me like two drowning people pulling each other down. I think we need the opposite. We need to, you know, buoy each other up, if we can. Regardless, our difference of opinion has made it really hard for us to sympathize with each other."

"I can imagine it must be extremely difficult."

"It is. And I don't think I want to talk about it anymore."

"All right."

"I mean ever. With anyone."

"That's your choice."

"We'll see what Culver has to say about that."

"What do you want to talk about instead?"

"You called us friends earlier," Blue said, parting their hands but locking their eyes. "Are we friends?" Fir could not determine whether Blue's tone suggested they should be more or less than that.

The segue was sudden, and unexpected, even though Fir had been waiting for a scene like this for years. A lick of flame leaping up from dead embers. Had Blue's speech about Culver, about a failing marriage, been a way of justifying the transgression to come? Fir looked reflexively toward the white gold wedding band sitting pristine on Blue's finger and struggled to feel any moral concern for it at all.

"Why don't you tell me what we are," Fir said, at once evasive and provocative. "You tell me what you want, and I'll become that for you."

Their table was an insubstantial square, one of several lined up along a bench in the back of the diner. Their table was corner-most, only a slender foot away from the wall. Blue was settled on the bench, Fir was perched in the aisle chair.

"You're so far away. Come sit with me." Blue edged sideways a fraction to open up a narrow span between hips and wall. Fir slid into the scanty space, held on one side by Blue and on the other side by tiles, and dared a shy glance at Blue's eyes.

"I'm here," Fir said, aware of how banal, how literal the words sounded, wanting them to convey more, willing them to ascend in the alchemy of bodies, subtlety rising in the heat. *I am with you. I am yours.*

"Finally."

Blue's cheek was pressed against Fir's neck when the server came back around.

"Can I get you anything else?"

Blue's head, shaking no, jostled against Fir's jugular. "Just the bill, thanks," Blue said.

"I bet," the server replied, with a knowing smirk.

When the cheque came, Blue laid a $20 on top of it, waving away Fir's proffered cash.

"I don't want your *money,*" Blue said, and Fir said *ha,* a bit giddy because there was so little money to offer. Because it sounded like maybe Blue wanted something else instead.

In the car, after starting the engine, Blue turned to Fir and said, "I've never seen your apartment before."

SALAMANDER

The next time they met, after the diner, it was Fir who called.

"Do you want to come over?" Fir asked, suddenly and painfully aware of the persistence of adolescent awkwardness.

"I don't really—" Blue began.

Have time, think that's a good idea, want to? Fir silently supplied.

"Let's go for a walk," Blue said finally.

They drove to the same quaint town down the road from Euphoria, parked in a peaceful neighbourhood adjacent to the main street, and as they walked it occurred to Fir, belatedly, that Blue kept bringing them to that town so that they would not be seen by anyone they knew.

"I've done wrong by you," Blue said. That word—*by*—skittered like a lizard from rock to rock. *I've done wrong to you. I've done wrong through you.* It was a slither of disparate meanings that Fir could not quite catch. "I agreed to meet you today so I could apologize."

"You haven't done anything you need to be sorry for. Not to me, anyways."

"Not yet, but I'm about to; I'm saying sorry in advance." Blue paused, a moment of due silence for the mea culpa. "We can't see each other again."

"Stop," Fir said, halting abruptly on the sidewalk. "Don't turn this into something cliché."

"It's not a cliché." Blue stopped next to Fir. "Endings are just inevitable. That's why they can never be exceptional."

"Let me guess," Fir sighed. "You want to remind me that you're married. To explain that you weren't happy, and you fucked me so you could figure out whether your marriage still meant anything to you. It does. You don't need me because you never needed me."

"You're wrong."

"About what?

"It's not like that."

"Well, are you happy with Culver?"

"Yes."

"How can you be? You described yourselves as two people drowning."

"Culver is completely devoted to me." Blue paused. "To us," Blue added, or corrected.

Fir was offended. *Who could be more devoted than I have been?* "You're really, truly happy?"

Blue hesitated. "As happy as I can be."

"Are you sure?" Fir asked, in the way of someone wondering about being a vector to a greater happiness.

Harsh lines appeared all over Blue's normally soft face. "What would you know about anyone's happiness?"

"What wouldn't I know about it? Do you think that because I haven't been in a relationship for as long as you I can't possibly know anything about love? Is that it?"

"Why haven't you been? Maybe you should ask yourself that."

"I know exactly why and you do, too."

"What are you saying?" Blue asked.

"I'm saying that I've loved you all this time." Fir's brow was furrowed. "Ever since we met. No one else has meant as much to me."

"We're practically strangers," Blue choked out, incredulous or confused.

"What are you talking about?" Fir said. "I've known you for 20 years."

"No, you knew me once 20 years ago."

Sometimes, a sentence seems so true it becomes reality. *You knew me once 20 years ago.* Those words lay hard and cold as a paperweight on Fir's chest, with scraps of fantasy and an archive of memories faded and smudged by the years pressed beneath. A question, dripping fresh ink, hung over the sheaf ready to rewrite Fir's longest-held belief: *What does it mean to love someone who has become your acquaintance?*

Fir gazed up, field of vision expanding to take in the whole sky, trying to recognize how infinitesimal they both were, but it was useless because they didn't live in the clouds so there was no choice but to look down again and then Fir's eyes were filled with Blue, who was still standing there, immediate as ever.

"Blue…" Fir said. "Maybe you're right. Maybe we're strangers. I'd still give up my whole life for you."

"No one should be so unreasonable," Blue chided.

"Then I'm no one and I'm not here and nothing we do matters. This is just your lucid dream." Fir was motionless, barely breathing. "I'll do whatever you decide and I won't exist when you wake up."

"Do you just like things that are difficult?"

"This is only difficult for you. It's the easiest choice in the world for me."

"Right. What do you think we should do?"

"Look, I need a ride home. I promise I won't say anything,

I won't touch you, I won't even lay eyes on you. When you stop the car in my parking lot, I'll get out and start walking inside and if you want to go with me, you can and if you don't, then you won't even have to say no. You can just leave."

"Okay."

They were halfway back to Euphoria when Blue turned the car onto a deserted side street, parked on the desolate roadside where no one could see them but the trees, and slid onto Fir's lap.

"I don't feel the same," Blue said, fingers hooked into Fir's collarbone. "I wouldn't die for you."

"Why would I ask you to?" Fir replied, running a hand over Blue's hair.

CACHE

Three hours north of Euphoria by wing, there is a lake, vast as a sea, chrysocolla in the golden glow of sunlight but chalcedony in the sterling mist of an overcast day. Travellers reach its sandy beaches by highway, but the less popular stone-thick shores are only accessible by a two-lane road that ripples across the landscape like bedforms wrinkle the strands. Between the waterfront and the road are rows of trees, and an array of native plants: horsetails and harebells, pussy willows and porcupine grass—all those stalwart species that have survived being choked out by the encroaching unkindness of dog-strangling vines and the smoggy sprays of baby's breath.

One of the smallest of these rocky lakesides is, even now, presided over by a bird, the magpie, whose territory of five hectares comprises the entirety of that beach, as well as the bordering greenery.

That silver day, onto the magpie's shore, there came a human figure. It was the first of its kind since sunset the previous evening, and arrived, as they nearly all do, by car. This vehicle, gleaming like almandine, attracted the magpie's gaze. The figure was holding a shovel and cradling a shadow in its arms. It shot like an arrow to the part of the beach that was above the high-water line, at the edge of the trees, and there it dug a hole, a larger version of the kind the magpie makes with its beak to store food. Each time the human figure raised the shovel, light reflected from two rings on its hand.

"Then you were with me, now you are without me," the figure said to the hole it had just finished filling back in.

The magpie waited until the figure had left the beach before it swooped down to alight upon the spot where the shadow had been submerged in the sand. Pecking beak-deep, the magpie was disappointed to find no buried metal. Though it could not reach the buried shadow, the magpie knew now what the shadow was—knew it by the scent of human carrion still hovering in the air over the freshly-turned ground.

AERO

Fir stands numbly in the parking lot outside Utopia Video, staring into the empty dark of Thursday evening desolation in a small town, through which the kids must have ridden just moments before, until a sense of resolution flashes down like a beam of light from a UFO.

Fir thinks Fain would say it is a bad idea, but fortunately Fir believes that there is no objective measure of the merit of an idea, so the lack of a better idea means that this idea seems rather good and anyway Fain is not here. There are two main disadvantages to the idea, however: 17 minutes remain in Fir's scheduled shift, and, because Fir can no longer see the kids, that makes them difficult to follow. A phone call to Fir's only coworker, other than the store owner, goes unanswered, so Fir leaves a note on the door and makes a wordless appeal for no trouble before locking up the store.

A lone, gangling youth on an unlit bike comes into murky view on the road ahead just before the sign for the trailer park does. *The Singing Frog,* the sign announces, though the image is evidently a rendering of a green toad, its skin nodular and mossy, its body stocky and its nose broad. Fir stops pedalling and the tires' frantic whine quiets to an insectival whir, indistinguishable from the ambient sounds of the summer night. It could be the taller kid—*Limn?*—from earlier. Certainty is impossible but probability is high as the biker turns. Breaching the driveway into the park several seconds after the teenager does, Fir flicks off the handlebar light, cringing at the unavoidable crackling of gravel beneath bike tires. The teenager, seemingly unaware of the noise, does not look back. Fir casts glances in several directions, scouting for Limn's short associate—*Mal?*—but there is no one else about.

As an adolescent, equal parts judgmental and jejune, Fir had held a view of trailer parks that was both grotesque and romantic, seeing them as a kind of trash bacchanal. Bonfires that burned all night, threatening to come uncontained. Laughter rollicking over acres. Punch-drunk colours of patio lanterns and string lights. The trailer park had once marked the raucous margin of Fir's entire existence. It was a borderline, the other side of which promised only the homeless hitchhiking of the highway life, or death in the county cemeteries.

Now Fir envies these people who live in houses they own on land they don't, homes they can mostly take with them if they want to leave. There is a decided appeal to retaining familiar walls while the views outside the windows change. Adulthood, prior to the current apartment that Fir clings to furiously, was spent in a series of short-term housing arrangements, some small as single rooms. Any continuity Fir could hope for had been a single bed and assorted ephemera, including one particularly ironic artifact from childhood—a silver spoon whose handle is engraved with a hummingbird.

The biker passes through the electric sunshine of a bare yellow LED bulb outside the trailer park's management office and Fir recognizes the hoodie. It is indeed Limn. What luck—the very person who may have seen something important. With relief, Fir observes that the inside of the management office is darkened, for though Fir is adamantly following a lead, not a child, appearances might suggest otherwise.

Just past the office, Limn lets the bike fall to the ground and hops a fence to sit cross-legged at the edge of the closed pool, staring into the water without touching it. Distant lights make visible the rippling surface, which gleams aero, a colour that is in fact more green than it is blue. Fir comes to a gradual stop, landing tender-footed on the grass at the edge of the drive and concealing both self and bicycle behind a nearby trailer whose windows are curtained and dim.

As tongue turns to leather, and bladder begins to pinch, and feet inflame with pinpricks of pain, and eyelids falter and fall, Fir fidgets almost imperceptibly, speculating about how long Limn is likely to maintain this melancholic posturing.

After more than an hour, the teenager finally leaves the poolside, picking up the bike but not getting back onto it, leading it like a pony, while Fir tiptoes behind. They follow the curving path further into the trailer park—which is as subdued as any suburban street at night, contrary to Fir's childish superstitions—before stopping at a fifth wheel travel trailer that towers twice as high as the pickup truck parked adjacent to it. Bike locked outside, Limn goes into the trailer, leaving Fir standing alone in the dark with a newly forming awareness of the realities of trailer park life. Fir is incapable of fully appreciating this education, preoccupied with the frustration of having discovered nothing yet about the bones. Overhead, a jet brushes a glimmering streak across the sky, much too impatient to be a star and far too lethargic to be a meteor.

CRYPSIS

After a long footslog through the Unwood, the road leading home sucks at Slip's boots, sloppy as quicksand, each step like carrying a jalopy. Quicksand, contrary to what much of cinema would suggest, is not a killer, but is, sometimes, the pentobarbital that soothes the limbs to stillness before pancuronium bromide and potassium chloride sweep in to pull life from the body, like tides carrying away debris. Pancuronium bromide is a curious name for a lethal drug, with its incidental echoes of *pan* and *cure,* as though it were a synonym for panacea, which, perhaps, death is in some sense. Potassium chloride, the second agent of death, is the salt of ancient lakes, to remind us of the danger of that same substance—water— that makes a body whole. Quicksand is not a killer; it holds the torso down while waves do the work of drowning.

The path through The Singing Frog is called Winder's Way, and Slip trudges along the edge of it, arms slightly outstretched and wavering, like the limbs of a wind-thrown sapling that is too small to hold even the nightjars, those featherweight birds who are cryptic, aerial, sifting the surrounding twilight for insects.

Nearly home, Slip almost stumbles over someone lurking behind a darkened trailer and peering around the corner of it, seemingly to observe the well-lit neighbouring trailer. Slip takes several regretful steps back, like an actor retreating stage-side after a castmate has stolen a few lines. A costume sewn of camouflage, a buttoned lip—these performative tricks are supposed to belong to Slip and the nocturnal birds, but here is a stranger out and about in their park, in their darkness, using the same tactics. It is insulting, and a little unsettling. Slip can think of nothing to do except to keep quiet and hidden and wait to receive more information about the situation.

The stranger, still and watchful, begins to grow moss, transforming into a fixture of the landscape. Waiting for what? Slip, exhausted, resolves to become obvious without being seen, and throws a pebble, which pings against the trailer where the shadowy stranger is half-concealed. The stranger startles, and makes a frantic but cursory reconnaissance of the darkness, before returning to the point of obsession.

There is a crackle of gravel. Slip discerns a third set of footsteps approaching them both from behind, and so recedes between two trailers, reemerging partway only after this unidentified third person has passed. Distantly, a key clinks in a lock, and a door thuds closed. The lurking stranger, finally jolted by this close call, goes back the way Slip and the third person came, gliding soundlessly past Slip's hiding place and following Winder's Way toward the trailer park's exit.

Slip wants to go to bed, or at least sit down, but continues to wait in apprehension of further potential surprises. After several moments' stillness, it seems safe enough to proceed. In the window of the lit trailer the stranger had been watching, Slip sees the silhouettes of an adult and a child, facing each other in ordinary conversation, and Slip supposes that the watcher might have been an estranged parent or spouse.

Finally back at home, Slip surveys window screens, tests doors, takes inventory of bare valuables, and lifts and then lowers the sheet that covers the bones on the couch like a shroud. Slip is relieved to find that the fragile frame of security is intact.

"We're safe," Slip says to The Corpses, retrieving that morning's teabag from a saucer to brew a second cup. "I'm glad."

Slip sits at the kitchen table, resting both head and forearms on its steady surface. Blanketed as they are, talking to The Corpses feels as ordinary as speaking to people who are asleep. "When I first lived here, I was always afraid the trailer would be broken into. It's not as big and intimidating as a house. It felt vulnerable, like a bird's nest. Like anyone could come and pick it up and take all of its contents away from me. One fell swoop, all my tiny chicks. Ha ha. As you can guess, that didn't happen. No, I soon realized I was more likely to die of a heart attack and not be found 'til my rent came due."

Slip trudges to the bedroom, sinks into bed, mutters into the pillow so The Corpses can't hear. "But you're here now, and I've got more than myself to think about."

ZERO

Fir hung up the phone after the call went to Blue's voicemail for the second day in a row, thinking it might have been wrong to call again, might even have been wrong to call the first time. When the second call had initially gone through and there was the sound of ringing, the hope of answer, Fir had stopped pacing, but afterwards resumed, footfalls cadenced as a clock.

"What else could I have done?" Fir addressed the empty room, whose walls were pale, expressionless, inoffensively blank. A single bed with an untucked cotton sheet, formerly navy, now more of a vague slate, was the only addition, but it alone crowded the room, made the space feel smaller than it already was.

Would you please just tell me if you're okay? Fir threw the words like seeds into the text field and then scrambled to grab them all back. *Can you tell me you're okay?* Another repossession. *Are you okay?* A final revocation. There was no definite reason to suppose that Blue was not perfectly fine, as far as living things went, life being suffering, etc. What could Fir say?

Outside, summer went on uninterrupted. Clover populated the boulevards, gulls combed the sidewalk for orts of food escaped from garbage cans. A block from home, Fir considered returning to the apartment for the phone and calling Fain, who perhaps would have something sensible to say. But Fir already knew what such good sense would entail and did not want to hear it.

There was a letter in the pocket of Fir's jeans, and Fir's index finger found it, pressing the ragged corner of it. No need to remove a piece of paper whose contents were already committed to memory. The letter had arrived one week prior, and for five days Fir had kept duly silent, conscientiously reading and rereading the letter, patiently waiting for the paper to reveal a palimpsest that controverted the final plain meaning of the text.

Fir intended to choose directions arbitrarily, to walk the city only to keep the feet busy and oblige the mind to consider something, anything, other than its sole fixation. Fir tried hard to observe the landscape carefully and thoughtfully. There was the sky (blue), and a mailbox (blue), and a dog's collar (blue), and forget-me-nots (brilliant, striking blue). All the while, Fir's mind, with its scheming subconscious, was leading Fir's feet circuitously but surely toward Blue's house. Once Fir noticed the deception, it became obvious that, without a wilfully imposed purpose, both mind and body would fall back into base desire.

Forgoing the usual polite call ahead, Fir changed route and showed up unannounced on Fain's doorstep. A roommate answered and left to get Fain, who appeared in the door moments later.

"Oh no, did I forget we were hanging out?" Fain asked, all solicitous concern.

"We didn't have plans or anything," Fir replied reassuringly. "I just wanted to talk to you and happened to be in the neighbourhood."

"Oh, okay. Well, do you want to come in?"

"Yes please."

A haphazard cairn of footwear filled the mat, so Fir's shoes took an empty space on the adjacent floor.

"Most of my roommates aren't around, so we can sit in the kitchen for once," Fain said. "It's a lot bigger than my room."

Indeed, the kitchen was spacious, airy, wallpapered with an old, cheerful print covered in daisies. Fir and Fain sat at the large, light red oak table, and their glasses of iced soda effervesced with fervour.

"I haven't seen you in a while," Fain said. "How've you been?"

"Yeah, all right, I guess. I mean, some things have happened since we saw each other last. But I'm fine, on the whole. How are you?"

"Oh, you know. Work. Hobbies. Occasional weekend out. What things?"

"Actually, that's what I wanted to talk to you about. I need your advice." Fir paused, indecisive. Fain, who was the veteran of one marriage and countless informal relationships, yet managed to never appear consumed by any of them, seemed like the ideal person to answer Fir's query. "There is this person, we were friends—no, more than friends, but not lovers, I guess I wouldn't call us lovers— I mean we were young, we spent all our free time together, and I thought we could just go on like that forever, but of course you can't. People grow up, get jobs, change cities, have kids, whatever. They are drawn apart. This person did get a job, and did marry, and tried to have kids, so we hardly saw each other for years. Many years. Then, about a month ago, this person called me, wanted to talk, so we talked, and within a couple of weeks we were, shall we say, *entangled,* in a way that married people are not supposed to be entangled. Of course, there was some concern about that, on both sides, but we kept ending up together anyway. It felt inevitable. Then last week I found this letter in my mailbox." Fir unfolded the letter and laid it on the kitchen table, as though it were a precious lost manuscript page recently recovered. Fain read it without touching it:

I have already chosen a life.

In the silence of Fain's concentration, Fir inwardly recited the lines of the letter yet again, beginning to worry that it might have been a miscalculation to reveal a document so intimate—to anyone, let alone to Fain, who, while a good and reliable friend, had rarely been a confidante, since Fir typically had nothing to confide.

The roles have been assigned and they limit what you and I can be to one another.

Perhaps Fain did not feel as invested in Fir's personal life as the disclosure of such an emotional record presumed.

Though we will not speak again, be sure of how much you have meant to me.

Maybe Blue's confession was made in absolute confidence and so this act of sharing constituted a betrayal.

You were my last great surprise.

What would Fain do if Fir calmly removed the paper from the table before the ending could be read?

Blue xx

Fain finished reading, looked up, scrutinized the expression on Fir's face. Neither of them seemed willing to be the first to speak.

"So this person," Fain said.

"Blue."

"Blue, okay. This person gave you this letter a week ago."

"Yes."

"And you have not heard anything further since then?"

"No. And I tried calling twice but there was no answer and I didn't leave a message."

"Right." Fain sat in wordless thought for a while again,

eyes fixed absently on the letter. "There are worse ways to be broken up with," Fain said finally.

"Like what?" Fir asked.

"I once had a valentine whose last words to me were *FUCK YOU DON'T CALL ME,* written in bright yellow chalk on the sidewalk below my bedroom window."

"How did you know it was for you?"

"We'd just had a pretty big fight the night before, in which I was told that my childish unwillingness to move in together was malicious, disrespectful, and probably pathological, to which I responded that only a child needs to be tucked in every night."

"The message still could have been for someone else."

"Regardless, I didn't call, and my sweetheart never called me again either. So even if the words were originally intended for someone else, they were still meant for me in the end. But enough about the minor intrigues of my dating life. I assume you had a reason for showing this to me."

"You already answered my question without realizing it, I think. I keep wanting to see this as something other than a breakup note, but, that's really all there is to it, isn't there?" Fir asked.

Fain smiled pityingly. "You know this person better than I do."

"But your perspective is clearer and less biased."

"On the contrary. My perspective is more distant and therefore my vision is more blurry."

"That was the first thing you said though. You called it a breakup."

"Yeah, okay, but I'm not a philologist. Don't take my interpretation as definitive."

"Who else can I ask? I'm not supposed to talk to the very person who wrote this note."

"Doesn't that tell you all you need to know then?"

"What if it's not a breakup? What if it's a cry for help?"

"What makes you think it would be a cry for help?"

"*You were my last great surprise.* That sounds ominous, doesn't it? Someone who says that is expecting to never be surprised again, which suggests to me that either the person is really depressed or expects to die soon."

"And you want to disobey a dying person's last wish? Or do you think you're going to cure someone of depression by destabilizing a home life?"

"I knew you would say that."

"But you asked me anyway."

"I don't have anyone else to ask," Fir said and Fain's lips rolled inward, like snails retreating into their shells.

When Fain rose, Fir expected to be shown the door but instead Fain went to the cupboard, rummaged around, retrieved a crinkly bag, let loose a cascade of small objects that danced daintily, *tap tap tap,* as they hit the bottom of a ceramic bowl, and set the bowl in the middle of the table. Pretzel twists.

"Are these supposed to be symbolic?" Fir asked.

"If you want them to be," Fain said lightly. "When was the last time you ate something?" Fir shrugged noncommittally. Fain went to the counter and came back, bringing a single object to the table, holding it in midair until Fir opened a palm to receive it.

"A conference pear," Fain said, and Fir took the fruit and laughed for the first time that day. "Let's pretend for a moment that this really is a cry for help," Fain continued. They both looked down at the note that still sat innocuously between them, as if verifying that it had not blown away, that the words upon it had not been spontaneously transformed. "What would you do?"

"Call Blue, again. Leave a message this time."

"Do you think that will solve whatever the problem is?"

"I suppose not. Whatever it is, though, it's probably more than a simple error of communication between us."

"Okay, so you call and you talk and it does not solve the problem. Or you call and leave a message and your call is not returned. What then?"

"I would go to Blue's place."

"Where Blue lives with a spouse."

"Yes, with Culver, who may not even be there, but could be out, or working. Who can say?"

"So you show up unannounced at the house of your former *paramour,* whose spouse is conveniently away. And then?"

"We talk. I find out what's wrong. I see if I can help."

"What can you do that Culver can't?"

"Maybe Culver is the problem."

"Maybe, but wouldn't that make you the worst possible helper? You're more likely to inflame the situation further because of your," Fain paused, "compromised position. Your involvement could make things *worse* for Blue."

"What if I'm the only one who can help? Then it doesn't matter if I'm the worst helper because bad help is better than no help at all." Fir was conscious of sounding like a character in an after school special. However, being unable to access an operatic register, felt that it was the only relevant script at hand given the melodrama of the whole situation. "What if things *have* to get worse before they can get better?"

"There are nearly 8,000,000,000 people in the world. Surely, *surely,* there is someone who might be of use to Blue apart from you."

"When a flower is dying, all raindrops are the same—

only the sun is irreplaceable."

Fir startled at the sound of an unfamiliar voice intruding upon their presumption of privacy.

"Hi," the voice said, its body now coming into view and extending a hand to Fir. "I don't think we've met."

"This is our newest roommate," Fain explained.

"Hey," Fir said, choosing that word because of its ambivalent echoes of both greeting and protest.

"So are you the rain or the sun?" the new roommate asked Fir, opening the fridge and inspecting its contents at length.

Fir was loath to admit to being mere precipitation but, sitting at the kitchen table, humdrumming fingers upon it in consternation, glooming like a rain cloud, there was no other answer that could be convincingly given. It was preferable to say nothing.

"Don't mind our resident poet," Fain said.

"I won't mind," Fir said, which could imply *I will not be upset,* but just then meant, *I will pay no attention.*

"Having a hard day?" the new roommate inquired, choosing the incorrect meaning from the possible two options and then snapping open a pop can for emphasis.

"Yes, it's been a hard day," Fir said curtly, fully meeting the eyes of the new roommate—just visible over the lid of the can—for the first time. "Someone died."

In an instant, a sound came from the new roommate's throat that made Fir think of a baby bird gurgling and choking on an over-sized morsel of worm. The new roommate emitted a single, short cough and quickly swallowed down both soda and shock.

"Oh fuck. I'm sorry. I shouldn't have asked. I wouldn't have asked if I'd known. Fuck. That's terrible." Slight panic suspended the new roommate's face in a tense and wide-eyed stare, but Fir suspected that, beneath the glaze of fear, there was a crack in the ceramic from which filthy water would spill if the surface did not hold. In other words, Fir suspected that, given the least opportunity to relax, the new roommate would go right on asking afflictive questions. *Who died? How did it happen? Can I touch the cadaver?* Fir, therefore, maintained a resentful glare.

"We were actually just going to move our conversation to my room before you came in," Fain said. "A communal kitchen isn't really a good place for a discussion like this."

The new roommate just nodded, perhaps held wordless by Fir's unrelenting scowl.

"Come on," Fain said, patting Fir on the back in an uncharacteristically parental way.

"Actually, I think I'll go," Fir said, palming the pear that had lain neglected on the table. "Thank you for the fruit."

"Goodbye." The new roommate offered a dazed wave.

"I'll walk you out," Fain said through clenched teeth.

When they reached the sidewalk, Fir and Fain stopped and stood facing each other.

"Someone *died*," Fain parroted incredulously.

"Well?" Fir hissed. "That's what I'm afraid is true."

"Is it so hard to believe that you were just plain and boring broken up with?"

With a shake of the head, Fir turned and walked away.

"Where are you going?" Fain shouted.

"I'll tell you later."

"Don't do anything foolish!" Fain added, a little plaintively.

Fir did not reply.

Children billowed over the sidewalks, boisterous and slow on their way home from school. So much of the day had passed. Fir did not want to be walking to Blue's house in the late afternoon, those terrible hours when the twin spectres of family dinners and living room repose come within sight, but there was no better choice. It felt impossible to conceive of an entire evening spent at home, alone and worrying.

This is not foolish, Fir thought. *A fool is an entertainer. No one even sees what I'm doing.*

Down the street from the intended destination, before the facade of Blue's house was even yet visible, Fir stopped. Culver was standing in their driveway, washing a blood-red convertible. Culver glanced up, but Fir turned away before their eyes could catch.

"I couldn't go through with it," Fir said, back at Fain's kitchen table.

"You probably did the right thing," Fain replied, and Fir considered whether that hedge was a careful evasion of a gloat, or whether it revealed a lack of conviction that was there the whole time.

The front door opened and there was shuffling in the hallway. From the kerfuffle, the new roommate emerged, calm on the threshold of the kitchen for a fraction of a second before registering that an antagonist had returned unexpectedly.

"Oh!" the new roommate said to Fir. "Hello again."

"You're back," Fain responded, when Fir did not say anything.

"I'll leave you to it," the new roommate muttered, retreating quickly from the room.

"Now what will you do?" Fain asked Fir once faint strains of music from the new roommate's stereo had wended their way down the stairs.

"I guess I'll cry," Fir replied, eyes distant and dry.

LINGER

Beneath the heather veil of rain that fell the following morning, the street leading to Blue's house appeared only distantly related to the place that Fir had walked just the day before. It was nearing 11:00 a.m., so the early migration of schoolchildren and day workers was over, and their noontime movements had not yet begun. In the interim, no one was parting the silver chill of mist to seek leisure. That was as Fir would have it.

Years had elapsed since the last planned visit to Blue and Culver's house, yet Fir did not think of that, did not register the absence of cars in the driveway, in fact noticed hardly anything about the surroundings, but walked purposefully to the door, knocked three times in staccato succession, and listened only for the anticipated sounds from the other side.

The rain stopped while Fir stood on the porch, waiting for the door to move.

BAD AS IT COULD BE

"This is terrible," Fir said to Fain as they sat on folding lawn chairs on the deck of the house in which Fain rented a room. Since the rain ended, the postliminary sun had been scorching, and the aluminum exposed between the chairs' strips of polypropylene webbing was accumulating heat. Now it seared the skin whenever Fir fidgeted and subjected a fresh strip of flesh to its burning touch.

"Is it?" Fain asked.

"Truly as confusingly bad as it could be."

"Explain."

"There's nothing else I can do, is there? I've visited. I've done the one grand gesture I was putting off and it accomplished nothing. I still have no idea whether Blue is in trouble. Am I supposed to show up every day like some kind of stalker? Obviously I can't do that. For all I know Blue was home but saw it was me and hid. It would be awful of me to just keep going back and back and back. So now I have to wait in suspense, possibly forever. There might very well be no end to this. I could just go on every day until I *die* not hearing anything from, or about, Blue."

"If you'd done as I suggested, you could still have that ace up your sleeve."

"You mean I could still be living in the ignorant hope of resolution."

"Yeah. But you didn't listen, so here we are, in the ignorant despair of irresolution."

"Ugh," Fir sighed, eyes closed against the glare of sunlight. "Let's not speak of it anymore. What about you? Tell me what's going on in your life."

"Caring about other people really is one of the most practical forms of escapism," Fain said evasively.

But Fir did not think of caring about Fain as a mode of escapism—not a flight on jewel-bright wings away from the self. Rather, Fir felt that focusing on Fain would be a way of transferring concern from Blue, a person who did not want Fir's concern, to Fain, a person who might come to appreciate it in time.

AMONGST FRIENDS

Limn understands the importance of canvas, even a simple cotton duck canvas stretched over cheap, light pine and primed with a layer of white latex paint. Last year, Limn received just such a canvas as a birthday gift, and immediately wrapped it back in the robin's egg blue tissue paper it came in, emptied a drawer, and placed the wrapped canvas inside, taking it out only occasionally since then to run fingers across the surface, smooth but for an ever-so slight toothiness, a subtle and delicate catch, like touching corn silk or lanugo. Limn is waiting for the right subject, one that obviously deserves this single, perfect surface.

Until then, there is paper. Artist sketchbook paper on a good day, lined notebook paper when the day is less auspicious. Acrylic paint warps the thick, loose paper of a sketchbook, but it bleeds right through the thin sheets of a notebook so that Limn has to fold newsprint and lay it between each page to keep the paintings from dissolving into each other. Now and then, on the best days, there is wood, whatever Limn can salvage—offcuts of raw lumber left to the trash, or stained handicrafts at yard sales that can be bought for a quarter and painted over.

Today is a sketchbook day, a minor luxury Limn allows

as a salve for loneliness. With the parent gone to work and the friend at a party with people Limn does not wish to make the acquaintance of, it is all, if not strictly normal, still quite close to normal, and should not be a big deal. The sense of abandonment is too much though, for whatever reason; Limn's teenage moodiness perhaps, or something else that is probably fleeting and does not bear extensive analysis.

On the paper, a frog begins, daub by daub, to materialize. Frogs, those solitary creatures rarely seen together. This one is a Gray Treefrog. The name is misleading, for Gray Treefrogs are not really grey, but a mottle of earth tones: mushroom grey, lichen green, the brown of dead leaves and fawns' hair. And even, on the underside of their legs, rarely seen, there is a shock of tangerine flesh.

With its lowered lids, this painted frog, half-submerged in water, looks like it is sleeping, but to Limn it is eating, pushing its bulging eyes back inside its own body to help move a praying mantis down its throat. Before being swallowed, the praying mantis would have been swimming, an odd behaviour for a land-living insect, but what is stranger to Limn is the fact that praying mantises can swim at all. Around the frog, the water is bubbling, as if it is boiling. But it is not. The night water is satiny and cool against the frog's skin, and the bubbles are only a sign that, beneath the surface of the pond, too far away for the frog to hear them, there are fish swishing their fins in a frenzy of affection for one another.

JUST ONE MORE

"I could try just one more time though, right? That wouldn't be too weird. It's been two weeks since I went to Blue's house and I only went the once."

Fir and Fain stood on opposite sides of the Utopia Video counter—Fir was behind it, setting nickels and quarters free from their paper rolls and watching them tumble into the expanse of the cash register drawer, while Fain was in front of it, deliberately disarraying the brick-stacked bubblegum and candy bars.

"Do what you have to do, I guess," Fain said finally.

"Thanks, Superego."

"You're welcome, Id Kid."

"Working today?"

"I was called in for a night shift yesterday. Had to run some errands around here afterwards so I thought I'd stop by and see you, then I'm going home to bed."

"This is your current security guard job?"

"Yeah, the one where I'm like a substitute teacher for buildings abandoned by their usual guards. I hope it lasts for a while so the temp agency doesn't give me another catering gig.

Security work is so peaceful."

Fir wondered if it was the relative loneliness of the job that made Fain so eager to see people socially outside of work.

"I'm sure you understand what that's like." Fain pointedly surveyed the bare aisles. "This place is almost as lifeless as an office building after dark."

"You're always in here at our least busy times." Fir glanced self-consciously around the empty shop floor.

"I think you prefer it this way," Fain said appraisingly. "The store changes slowly, some movies come and go, while the old classics stay on the shelves year after year. It's always morphing and always familiar, at the same time."

"A paradox. Like how movie theatres let you be close to other people without ever speaking."

"Both too quiet for me, but they suit you I guess. What I enjoy about temp work is that I rarely have to remain in the same spot for long. I couldn't stand going back to the same room every day for years. No offence."

"Yes, it's funny, isn't it? You're the security guard but I'm the one who wants job security."

"Ha ha." Fain feigned laughter. "Job security is a myth. There are shorter jobs and longer jobs and you never know which you have until you're fired."

"You should give up temp work and become an economist."

"Actually, I think I might give up temp work to become a therapist."

"I'm going to choose to ignore that."

"You are the harbourmaster of your feelings. Do not give in to the waves. Trust in the sanity of your ship."

"Isn't it past your bedtime yet?"

"You're right," Fain said, jangling car keys. "Have fun dusting shelves without me."

Amid the fragile echo of the doorbell chime, Fir tried to name a friend, any friend, besides Fain, who Fir had talked to in the past few weeks, but could not conjure a single figure.

Later that day, astride a bike and obscured by dusk in the parking lot of the police station, Fir watched people go in and out of the low-rise building, trying to discern whether they were confident in the rightness of being there.

After emerging from the building an hour later, Fir rode down the street and stopped in a parking lot a few blocks away to make a call.

"Miss me already?" Fain asked.

"I went to Blue's house again—I know, I know—and there's a buildup of mail in the box, the grass is overgrown, there are no cars in the driveway, and no one will answer the door. I even went in the evening this time, after I got off work, when Blue, or Culver, or both, are most likely to be home. So I went to the police station and tried to report them as possible missing persons to the police but the officers—I spoke to two of them, they both got annoyed with me—just kept asking me what my relationship was to them, how close I was, would I even be told if they went on vacation? I asked: *What if one of them killed the other?* Well, that was a ridiculous question, apparently. They laughed at me. They said, and I quote: *There are no murders in Euphoria.* I said: *Murder can happen anywhere.* The officers looked at each other and shook their heads. *Furthermore,* they said, *do you know the current statistics on spouses killing each other? It's a phenomenon so uncommon it's practically non-existent. They just break up when they're ready to move on.*

"And, statistically, they're right, so I thought maybe I should tell them about everything that happened, show them the letter, but I was worried that they would think I was some jealous ex, not actually concerned about their welfare, you know, so I didn't mention any of that, do you think I should've? Oh, it doesn't matter now, I can't go back in there, then they really won't take me seriously, maybe they'd even get suspicious of me, I don't know. What do I do now? I've done the absolute last thing I wanted to do, the last thing I could think of to do, but the police won't even investigate it, they thought I was just in there wasting their time or something, as if I would've gone at all if I could've avoided it—"

Fain interjects. "I'm going to stop you there for just a second. I get why you're panicking and I'm sorry the police didn't help, but maybe let's not do this over the phone. Where are you right now? I'm going to pick you up and we can talk through a plan for what to do next."

"I'm in the parking lot of that wholesale furniture store near the police station. You must've seen it, it's the one with the 20-foot tall inflatable palm tree out front."

TEST SPECIES

At two in the morning, there's a knock on the trailer door.

"It's me, let me in." The voice is hazy, hexing. Familiar under a wave of distortion.

Peering through the glass, Limn almost expects canine teeth crystalline as mountain peaks, but instead sees the top of Mal's tightly wound crop of hair, more disarrayed than usual, and unlocks the door. Mal whirlgigs inside, plucking a bag of corn curls from Limn's kitchen cupboard and pacing the floor with them.

"How was the party?" Limn asks.

"You should've been there," Mal replies through a mouthful of corn dust.

"But how was it?"

"Kinda boring, I guess but I did get high for the first time."

"You biked home stoned and alone at night?" Limn's tone is almost parental—irritated and protective.

"Oh, stop pretending to be an adult. You're taller than me, not older."

"Actually, I'm nine months older than you."

"Nine months, woooow. That's, like, not even one-fifteenth of our lives."

"Nine months is the difference between an invisible cell and an entire baby."

"Well, what'd a baby ever do for anybody anyway?" Mal stands on a chair in the kitchenette while Limn continues to hover cautiously near the door. "Did a baby ever make a beautiful piece of art? Did a baby ever feed a city? Did a baby ever save someone's life? No. I don't think so."

"Neither of us have ever done any of those things either."

"I like your paintings," Mal says. "But me? I'm nine months behind you. I'm basically just a single cell that isn't even its own organism yet."

"I have no idea what your point is."

"Did you find the gun yet?"

"What gun?"

"Maybe it was a knife."

"Who has a knife?"

"Maybe they went really old school and used a bow and arrow. Have you seen any gouged apples lying around?"

"I don't—"

"Target practice! Keep up, kiddo." Mal holds up a corn curl, mimes the arc of a throw. "Do you think your fish would like these?"

"No!" Limn crosses the room in a few sweeping strides to stand defensively in front of the sensitive neon tetras, who have almost disappeared into the vallisneria. They are only visible as glimpses of the oversized black marbles that are their eyes, or as glimmers of the red and blue that iridesce in parallel down the length of their lateral lines.

"Hopefully it wasn't a ligature." Mal's arm lowers. "That would be difficult. You think you're looking at a shoelace but really you're looking at evidence of a homicide."

"Is this about the bones?"

Mal sits down and begins layering corn curls on the table as if playing a block-stacking game, creating a precarious tower of unsaturated oil and processed grain.

"Did you go see them again while I was at the party?"

"No, I did not go visit the bones," Limn says, eyes rolling.

"Did you decide how you're going to handle that *volatile situation?*"

"I thought maybe I'd finish high school and then spend a couple years training to be a police officer and then get a job with the local station and slowly accumulate evidence in my spare time while I spend my working hours walking the beat until I am ready to bring charges."

"Hey." Mal points a cheese curl accusingly at Limn. "Don't get snarky with me."

"You started it."

"I'm on your side."

"How's that?"

"I support you by challenging you."

"Are you sure you're not just annoying me?"

"Mhmm," Mal nods. "You'd be boring without me."

"You mean I'd be bored with you."

"I meant what I said."

"What'd you take?"

"None of your business, narc."

"Okay whatever. Can we watch a movie now?"

"Yeah, all right. Which one?"

PINK SPIDERS

Morning sunbeams pour in through the windows of the trailer, which are uncovered because neither of the teenagers bothered drawing the curtains last night, but this is not what wakes Limn and Mal from their sleep, shoulders slumped against one another's on the foldout sofa. Rather, it is the clang of the trailer door opening that rouses Limn, who jostles Mal awake in the haste of rising, and it is only thereafter that both of them register their mistake, holding up their hands to protect their dilated eyes from the excesses of light—a reflex that precedes even their atavistic alarm, the frantic scanning of their habitat to determine the source of the loud, unidentified noise that woke them in the first place.

"Don't get up on my account," says a voice from the entryway, with a familiarity that calms the panicked slugs squelching their way through the synapses of the kids' slumberous temporal lobes.

"Morning," Limn says.

"Mmm," Mal choruses in pale imitation.

"Late night watching movies, I take it?" The television set is still on, images of the film menu looping ad nauseam.

"Yeah," Limn confirms, fully sitting up.

"Do you want breakfast? I can make some—" a kitchen cabinet opens, cans are pushed aside, restacked— "hash browns?"

"I'm not really hun—" Limn starts.

"Yes, we do," Mal intervenes.

"Good. It'll be nice to eat my dinner with company for once. Somehow my child is never hungry in the morning."

"I eat dinner with you when you work day shifts, and 'dinner' is at a normal time," Limn protests.

"I haven't worked days for months."

"That's not *my* fault."

"You can invite me over to eat anytime. All we ever have at my house is cereal," Mal puts in.

"You know you're welcome whenever you want. As long as you get here before ten, because that's when I fall unconscious."

"Invariably," Limn nods. "Like the opposite of a rooster."

"You're so lucky," Mal whispers loudly to Limn. "You get twice as much attention even though you have half as many parents as me."

"We can share," Limn offers, and Mal nods to seal the contract. From the kitchen, oil in the frying pan can be heard crackling like popcorn.

"Are you going to mention the—you know?" Mal asks.

"Maybe after you leave. There's no point in waiting, I guess."

Mal speeds through two-thirds of the hash browns, four pieces of toast with peanut butter, and a glass of apple juice, before disappearing out the door with a fifth piece of toast in hand.

"It worries me," Limn's parent says, holding out the last of the bread, "that you're a foot taller than that child and yet you eat so much less."

"I eat when I'm hungry."

"Do you want jam?" the parent asks, already layering marmalade over butter. Limn calculates the value of compliance.

"Sure." Limn takes the toast and bites off a placating mouthful of it, chewing slowly. "Can I ask you something?"

"Yes," Limn's parent replies, contemplating a mug nearly drained of decaf coffee so dark it is opaque.

"You have to promise you won't get me in trouble because of it."

"There is no way I am promising you that."

"Promise me you will try to be calm and fair and not freak out?"

"I'm not sure what it says about my parenting style that you feel the need to ask that, but sure, I swear I will try not to abandon all good sense when you tell me this thing. Though can I point out that this long introduction is making me very apprehensive about whatever it is you're going to say?"

"Hmm. I'll keep that in mind for next time."

"Next time?"

Limn pauses to consider, once more, the consequences of this confession. If Mal, the only person Limn has told about the bones so far, can be thought of as a test species—a water flea, a sheepshead minnow, or a mysis shrimp, animals chosen because they are small and easily observed, young because the young are the most sensitive of their kind—then the signs are grim. Yet, separate from any probability of success, Limn must also think of the possibly more dire potential effects of neglecting to say anything. If nothing is said, a murderer may persist. Limn knows that the police have not been to the trailer park because, whenever they have, gossip about their visit circulates as if diffused into the drinking water.

Surely, *surely,* Limn must say something to a trusted adult, like a parent. But is it enough that this parent is at home, sitting in the same room, eyes expectant? Is there another adult who could handle this better? The kind of confession Limn is about to make is not one of penance. It is not a gesture to assuage Limn's conscience, the sort of disclosure that can take place whenever the teller feels compelled. There must be a strategy guiding the approach. If the parent is not in a receptive mood, Limn's suspicions will be dismissed as the woolgathering of a fanciful adolescent mind that idles away its days in meadows of idyllic make-believe. It is unclear to Limn whether this is, or is not, that kind of time. What is obvious is that the parent is a grass carp with a bubbling gaze—far larger than a flea, or minnow, or shrimp—and Limn has disturbed the water with unnecessary movement. Limn has to say something.

"I'm sorry to inform you that Mal finished all your snacks."

ROAD TRIP

From the passenger seat, The Corpses mutter their discontents. Slip steers the old trailer with unsteady hands as it clunks and shudders over the country highway, every rut in the road jarring the bag of bones and making them complain. It is late afternoon, and the sun is poised above the edge of the windshield, almost ready to dip and slant directly through the glass. The trip had been no easier earlier with The Corpses on the floor. Or on the couch in the back. Or even stuffed into a cabinet, an indignity for which Slip had afterwards apologized profusely. No matter where they are, no matter the time of day, the bones will not be still or silent.

"Just a few more hours of driving before we stop, I figure." Slip is beginning to feel excluded from The Corpses' conversations and concerns. They exist in the private intimacy of that closed bag, a miniature home belonging to them alone, into which Slip can only occasionally peer like an outsider.

The Corpses clatter their reply.

"No, we can't stop before then. You know the rules. We only stay in places big enough that we won't be noticed. If we spend any time in a town so small it's only locals, people will see a little old person, travelling alone, in a big trailer packed with a lifetime of stuff. And they won't understand what we're doing. Won't see that there's a *we* here at all. And they'll get suspicious. That won't be good. We don't want that. I've already picked the next town we'll stay in. The campground is big, touristy. Perfect for us. We can disappear into a crowd of adventurers."

More click-clacking from the bones.

"I don't know what that's supposed to mean. Why do all your words sound the same?"

The next stretch of highway is smooth as they approach a larger town, so The Corpses' objections cease.

"Can't tell any of these gas stations apart," Slip complains as they pull off onto an exit. "Neverending pattern of brand names lining our highways." Not that any of the towns they pass look particularly distinct to Slip either, with all their houses stratified into neighbourhoods that each represent an obvious architectural era, the horizontal correlative of an archaeological dig. Older houses closer to the downtown, newer houses farther out, strip malls with the same sets of chain stores between them. But Slip will not mention such cynical observations to The Corpses, for whom this trip is supposed to be a sort of pilgrimage.

Inside the station, Slip pays for the gas in pocket change.

"Do you carry maps?" Slip asks the clerk, who gestures toward a half-empty stand of ragged paper. "Hmm." Slip casts an anxious, custodial glance toward the trailer, before perusing each of the maps in turn while the haggard attendant counts dozens of nickels and dimes. "These aren't what I'm looking for."

"All right. Do you want anything else?" the clerk asks, probably hoping for, if anything, a simple request for cigarettes or lottery tickets.

"You know what," Slip says, scrutinizing the clerk's face.

"Maybe you can help me. Are you from around here?"

"Uh, yeah. I mean I grew up near here."

"Ever been anywhere else? Gone abroad? Taken a cross-country road trip?"

"Just within, you know, the province. And I went on a cruise once for my honeymoon."

"Good. That's good. Okay, I'm going to ask you a question. Are you ready?"

"I think so?"

"Forget about your honeymoon for a minute. Pretend it never happened."

"Umm—"

"Tell me: where is the most beautiful place you have ever been?"

"I don't know. I guess I never really thought about it."

"Please try. It's very important."

"Okaaay," the clerk drawls incredulously, then sighs and stares up at the ceiling in concentration, as though a film of the past is playing there on fast forward. Slip offers privacy, turning away to face the station window. "Hmm, well…" the clerk hedges after a minute or more. "So I can't say this is definitely the most beautiful of any place I've ever been, but I can't remember any place that was more beautiful—will that do?"

"I'm going to write down my phone number," Slip says, copying it in black ink onto the corner of a free community newspaper, and handing it to the clerk. "Promise me you'll call me if you do remember a more beautiful place."

"Sure." Despite the tentative sound of that vow, the clerk dutifully tears off the phone number and pockets it.

"Now," Slip says, "what's the place you *do* recall?"

"Lac Lemot."

"Where's that?"

Pulling a map from the stand, the clerk's finger traces a line that staggers approximately north through the region.

"It's fate," Slip says. "That's the way we were already headed."

"Oh, I didn't know you had a crew with you." The clerk's tone offers a friendly *my mistake* that is followed by confusion when the clerk looks out the window and sees no one in the passenger seat of Slip's trailer.

"We're meeting up later," Slip says quickly, checking the time. "In about ten minutes, in fact! I'd better hurry. Thank you."

A strident chime above the gas station door automatically remarks on Slip's abrupt departure.

"I was going to buy the map," Slip tells The Corpses as they pull out of the station. "I was going to remind the clerk, *call me if you remember a more beautiful place,* but then I thought, no, better not to draw more attention to us. It was bad enough that I mentioned you at all. No offence."

The Corpses make use of the next pothole to voice their complaint.

CLOVER

At a gas station on the other side of town, Slip pulls over even though the tank is full, and buys a map of the region just like the one that was left behind.

"Let's see," Slip mumbles when back in the trailer, perhaps addressing The Corpses and perhaps not. "Page 23. Square 7-C. Luck luck luck." Now Slip turns purposely toward The Corpses, tilting the map to face them. "What was I thinking? That won't do you any good. You're in a bag. Right, so you can't see it but I estimate it's about 150 kilometres from here to the lake. We won't actually go to the lake today, but we will go a bit farther than I originally planned. It looks like there's a campground," Slip taps a spot on the map where a triangle sits like a hat on a green amoeba of land, "in a town just south of the lake. We can stay there tonight and go to the lake tomorrow. I know, I know, that means at least another couple of hours of driving. Yes, probably more like three hours because it's mostly two-lane roads, a lot of stop and go. Hey, at least you don't have to drive. Do you think these old wrists appreciate such a rough ride? Yeah, okay, fine, you're *all* bones with no tendon or muscle or anything to cushion the shock for you, and all right,

I admit I don't know how old you are either. We can sympathize with each other though, can't we? Let's leave it at that."

Most of the campground they stay in that night is populated by tents: lightweight green nylon for the backpackers, polyester sprawling in bold blues for the families, and a handful of old stalwarts in bland shades of canvas that almost disappear into the scenery. Feeling conspicuous, Slip selects the lot at the far end of the trailer section—which sits between a massive RV and a row of trees— then backs up until the rear bumper touches the leaves.

"We got a nice, secluded spot," Slip says, turning off the engine but not unbuckling. "That trailer beside us is so big, you can tell they bought it because they don't want to ever have to get out of it. That's why there's no awning, no chairs, nothing outside, but it's got a satellite dish on top. Those are the neighbours you want to have if you're aiming to be left alone, all right. And no one has any reason to drive past us, except on the way out of the park. You don't have to worry too much about people who are on the way somewhere else."

At the end of the day, Slip likes to describe the sights that The Corpses have missed, euphemizing a little to make up for the fact that they have not witnessed them firsthand. Rows of tulips that were wilting in the park will perk up in Slip's retelling. Glossy slices of cheese extracted from thin plastic film will be replaced by thick wedges of hand-sliced cheddar when Slip recounts lunch. Occasionally, a three-leaf clover sprouts a fourth leaf. It is a performance of levity, and tonight the prospect of it exhausts Slip, who hopes The Corpses will not notice the omission.

"I have a surprise for you." It is a distraction for The Corpses, but also true.

The two chairs from the trailer's dinette are relocated to the grass of the lot. Obscuring darkness has emboldened Slip, who cautiously removes the rucksack of bones from the passenger seat and places it on the newer chair, where it reposes like a shadow among shades. Crouching in the grass, Slip tends to the fire pit, whispers to The Corpses, "Maple. Such a good hardwood for burning. When I saw that they had it at the office, I couldn't resist."

Feathery amber light wings out into the darkness. Settled back into the empty chair, Slip's words rustle, decibels below the faint sizzle of kindling. "I know you can't see much, but I thought you might be able to sense the warmth of a fire. Bet you'll feel it even more as it grows."

Children's giddy voices warble across the campground like wild bird call. An acoustic guitar sings in a major key. At this distance, when sight is blurred and sound is muffled, Slip can almost enjoy the noises that signify human life.

"This is just for me," Slip says, sliding a marshmallow onto the tip of a spindly twig. "Sorry. Don't think you'd like it much anyhow." The sugary skin caramelizes to a crisp shell that can barely contain the melting fluff of its milky guts.

"Actually, I love marshmallows." A disembodied voice issues forth from the inscrutable night. Rib bones, which Slip usually does not notice, begin to strain against the swelling of the heart.

"I wasn't offering one to you," Slip snaps back, covering a spark of fear with a blanket of anger.

"Who were you talking to, then?"

"The possums."

"Don't be offended." The words are laid over a percussion of footsteps. "I was just joking with you." Into the circle of firelight, an unfamiliar person steps. Younger than Slip by a good ten years, though not likely more. Taller by four inches at least. Slip tenses like a small animal in the presence of a larger one, even though there is no particular reason to be afraid.

"I don't like jokes," Slip says, deciding not to stand. Not yet. "I don't like company all that much either. Hope that doesn't offend you—it's nothing personal."

"All right now, I can tell where I'm not wanted. I was only trying to be friendly, but I'll let you be."

With one swift step, the face retreats from the circle of light, and Slip listens as the sound of crunching gravel slowly fades.

By midnight, most of the tents are darkened and there are few persistent sounds of activity, yet still, in the locked enclosure of the trailer, Slip cannot be calm. "What did that person want with us?"

No reply is forthcoming from The Corpses, who may or may not be resting, as living people do.

"I won't be able to sleep tonight," Slip explains. "That person might come back."

EVENSONG

Constant motion brings Slip an illusory sense of security. Out on the pitch-dark roads, too rural even for streetlights, there is hardly anyone around. The few cars they pass are hurtling toward their own version of purpose and want nothing to do with a ramshackle house on wheels. Hawk-looping the highways around Lac Lemot, Slip keeps them near their destination without quite reaching it.

"We'll close our eyes when the sun shines," Slip singsongs to The Corpses. That chorus carries them through until morning, when they are finally allowed to land.

BLOOM

An algal bloom in the waters of Lac Lemot looks more like spilled acrylic paint than a living organism to Slip, who stands on the shore amid the first rays of daylight, carrying The Corpses in the rucksack. The impression of toxicity that the bloom's blue-green brightness gives off is only intensified by the absence of visitors, and the schools of fish skeletons washed up on the beach.

"I heard it's because of the big farms around here—their fertilizers wash into the lake," Slip explains to The Corpses. "Algae just explodes. Then no one can go in the water, it's so full of bacteria." Cyanobacteria, specifically. "No one can know every secret hidden beneath a big lake like that."

Slip gazes into the water, whose depths are fathomless. "That's what my memory is like. The older I get, the deeper it feels, and all I can recall is whatever floats near the surface. I see my childhood like a series of photographs, or torn-out scraps from a journal. Flotsam on the waves. The details are missing. The immediacy is gone. Most days all I have left is the feeling that I'm forgetting something. Everything."

Slip shrugs it off and turns back to face The Corpses.

"Would you want to stay here for even five minutes? Yeah, me neither. This is not the place we're looking for. Not even close."

What, exactly, they are looking for, has never been clarified by Slip, and The Corpses have never asked.

ARE YOU DYING

Sleep is as untouchable as everything else for Limn, despite the previous night's lack. When finally the parent is asleep and, therefore, immune to worry—dreaming, probably, of neighbours separated by acres—Limn lightfoots it out of the trailer and into uncompromising morning. The sun has not relented, its heat intruding even through the rubber toes of sneakers. Despite knowing with near-certainty that Mal is at home, dozing off exhaustion, Limn remains on the qui vive, mistaking the lichen growing on a tree for Mal's mass of curls, the wing of a flitting wren for the glint of an ochre iris.

A gaggle of children approaches, zigzagging and jostling each other so they occupy the entire roadway. Grinding teeth, Limn drops off onto the grass, throwing a covert glance toward the pandemonium, defensively estimating the number of strides that would cover the distance between them.

"Hey!" one of them says to Limn. "What are you doing?"

"Walking," Limn replies.

"Walking where?" It is unclear whether this is the same child or another.

"Into town," Limn lies.

"Why?" a child asks. The first, the second, a third? It is like talking to an entire hive of bees.

"I'm going to the hospital." Limn expects this kind of solemn, adult disclosure to shut them up.

"Oh no, are you dying?" Evidently, that was a miscalculated tactic.

"Does that *look* like a person who's dying to you? Do dying people just walk around like *la la la I'm going into town now?*"

"How would you know what a dying person looks like? Who do you know who's died?"

"For your information, I had to watch my dog die."

"That—" a finger points pedantically in Limn's direction "—is not a dog. It's a person." *It,* Limn repeats inwardly. *It.* Like a pet name for an iteration, or a short form for itinerant. Limn wouldn't mind going by *It.*

"If you're so smart, why don't you explain to us all what exactly the difference is between a dog's death and a human's death."

How many children are there? Limn does not want to stare long enough to count them. In the turmoil of their argument, Limn hurries away without being given further notice.

Squeak, thud, click. That is how the door of the management office will shut, Limn foresees, and then there will be the cool, soothing static of the air conditioner. White noise like steady rain, or the engine of a car. *Hello, how can I help you?* the manager will say, purposeful and civil. Volume a necessity rather than an extravagance.

Reality inverts the order of Limn's fantasy. Approaching the office, Limn hears the manager first. The manager must be either on the telephone with a bad connection or quelling dissent with yelling. *You said our order would be delivered on Monday,*

Limn discerns. *It's August. What are we supposed to do without a stock of ice?* Second is the arrhythmia of the air conditioner, an elliptical sound from a circular swing. The door closing behind Limn chirps, a hesitant noise the manager talks straight through. "Don't just sit there and idly promise me a discount," the manager says. "What use is that. I expect a specified percentage. Yes. Yes I am asking in advance for the exact fucking number. That's hardly an exorbitant request."

Trailer park hearsay holds that the manager had once moved to a big city several hours away, spent six years at university, and dropped out midway through law school, either because of involvement in a student council embezzlement scandal on campus that could never be brought to trial for lack of evidence, or sentimental attachment to a dying parent who still resided in Euphoria. Watching the manager arguing heatedly over the phone, Limn can imagine the manager's parallel life that might have unfolded—a vociferous attorney bickering with a judge, indifferent to the fretful tittering of courtroom onlookers.

"Ten percent? Call me back when you change your mind." With a furious finger-tap on the cell phone screen that must feel unsatisfying, that must make a person nostalgic for the avoirdupois of a landline phone, the manager ends the exchange. "Straw boss. It sounds like an insult, doesn't it?" Limn is unsure of whether to answer this query. "Don't go into middle management, kid. Buy something and learn how to fix it yourself."

"Okay," Limn says. Does the manager own the trailer park? "Thanks." The manager, who has still hardly looked at Limn, spends a long while scrawling a note with a ballpoint pen. "I can come back later if this is a bad time," Limn offers.

"Now, later, doesn't matter. Life itself is a bad time."

Laughter drums from the manager, but not from Limn, who merely observes, bewildered. "What is it you want?"

"Actually, I've come to see you to discuss a matter of grave concern," Limn says solemnly. More disconcerting laughter from the manager. *Grave concern*—Limn resolves not to say that again, not to use any phrases that might be mistaken for wordplay, puns being the antithesis of the punctilious manner that Limn is trying to effect. But that can't be what the manager is laughing about, since the manager doesn't yet know that this visit concerns a dead body. "I'm serious," Limn insists. With a sigh, the manager flips to a fresh sheet of paper and holds a hovering pen over it, a jaded lawyer doing an intake with a less than auspicious new client.

"What's your name again?"

"Limn."

"Oh yeah, over in 6B. Just you and your parent."

"That's right."

"Okay, Limn. Tell me about this serious business."

How to begin? "I have noticed a series of suspicious occurrences." Limn ought to have rehearsed a speech beforehand. "Involving a long-time resident of the park." Get in all the credible details first, Limn figures, and wait to mention the bones, since they're the most difficult part of the story to believe. What else can be said, though? Subsequent events are only significant in view of that first cause: the discovery of the bones.

"First off, did any of this take place on park property?" the manager asks, saving Limn from further dawdling.

"Yes."

"Very well. We can proceed. Who is the resident?"

"Honestly…I'm not sure of the name. Skip, Snip, Ship, something like that. Anyway the person who lives in site 7A."

"Ah. The one who is currently away."

"You noticed that, too!"

"When a trailer leaves the park for the first time in decades, yes, I do tend to notice."

"Do you know why it happened?"

"Would I tell you if I did?"

"Is there rent owing?"

"How is that your business?"

"You don't know what's going on, do you? And you don't care because rent is paid."

Putting down the pen, the manager leans back in the chair, elbows on its arms, and appears to scrutinize Limn.

"Surely you didn't come here just to tell me that one of the residents is currently away from the park. And surely you didn't expect me to tell you why that's the case. So you might as well stop wasting time and tell me how any of this is suspicious and what makes you think I will care."

"Because there were human bones in 7A's trailer!" This admission, made without lead-up, without decorum, is not at all as Limn intended, and failure feels imminent.

Instead, the manager straightens attentively and shifts forward slightly, matching the posture that Limn has held since first sitting down.

"When were you in 7A's trailer? Under what pretext were you invited there?"

"I wasn't."

"I don't understand."

"I saw the bones through a window."

"Where were they?"

"In the trailer."

"No, I mean were they on the ground? On a table? Were they in proximity to any other objects of interest?"

"They were just sort of sticking out of the top of a bag."

"A body bag? A grocery bag?"

"Like a backpack. What are they called? The ones adults carry."

"A messenger bag?"

"Something like that."

"That sounds like quite the obstructed view."

"It was…" A pause. This time Limn waits for the right word to surface. "Sufficiently…" Yes. "Unobstructed." Not a graceful articulation, but adequately formal. Limn exhales.

"How do you know what human bones look like? What makes you think you can identify them?"

"I watch a lot of…documentaries."

"Oh, I see." The manager's neatly trimmed fingernails pulse against the arm of the chair, transmitting a series of rapid-fire sixteenth notes, like an indecipherable parody of a tap code. In Limn's peripheral vision, some kind of insect hurries along the floor and Limn's urge to track and identify it must be suppressed. "Television is quite educational these days, isn't it?" the manager asks.

"It can be."

In its former life, the portable that serves as the management office used to be a classroom, and it retains some of the atmosphere of its early years. Binders lining the shelves of the walls and a large, teacherly desk behind which the manager sits only reinforce this impression. Without moving from the hard plastic chair and its gaudy orange seat, Limn has somehow morphed from belligerent client to misbehaving student.

"What happened after you saw the bones?" the manager asks. "Were you observed?"

"I don't think I was. Nothing really happened at first, but then within a couple of days the trailer was gone from 7A. As if…"

"As if what?"

"As if someone was trying to hide something."

"Aha," the manager replies, though Limn cannot be sure what has just been revealed. Both of them startle in unison when the manager's cell phone rings. The manager picks it up and accepts the call. "Hello? Yes. I'll be with you in just a minute." The manager pushes a button and lays the phone face-down on the desk. "I do appreciate your concern for park safety, but Limn, you have to understand that I also need to respect the privacy of park residents. It is not appropriate to go sneaking around other people's trailers—neither for me, nor for you. Do you understand?"

"I understand." Rising, Limn means to leave, but stops. "I *understand* that you can't solve violence with, with—"

"Pedantry? Bureaucratic inertia? What is it you'd like to accuse me of doing or failing to do?"

"*Incuriosity.*" To Limn's surprise, the manager pens a brief message on the notepad, as if transcribing Limn's answer.

"Your assessment is noted. Now, if you don't mind being on your way, I have a call to take."

Giddy confusion buoys Limn on the walk home. Though the meeting is hardly to be counted a success, the reception from the manager was no worse than that of Mal. And if an unstaked acquaintance can be just as receptive as a friend who should be swayed by affection to believe what Limn says, then this suggests that there might someday be someone for whom these dangling observations, these flailing suspicions Limn harbours, will amount to something worth acting upon.

DECAMP

Northward, they drive again, Slip's eyelids faltering, lashes casting shadows on the road ahead. The sun has just fully breached the eastern horizon when they reach a town so populous it might even be called a city.

"Let's leave less to chance and not camp today."

In the motel office, the front desk attendant raises an eyebrow at Slip's trailer, parked right outside the door. "I guess you want a bit of luxury for a change?" the attendant asks.

"That's right," Slip says. Relic smells of cigarette smoke still cling to the office's burnt orange carpets. Embossed wallpaper that probably used to be gold has faded to a sheen of beige. The attendant hands Slip a room key.

As they settle into their room, Slip presses a hand into the mattress and remarks to The Corpses, "The bed in the trailer is just as good as this." Slip places the satchel, with The Corpses inside it, next to a corded telephone on a desk of ersatz dark cherry wood, then goes to the window and raps on it. "But the windows here are thicker. And the locks are stronger."

It is only early afternoon, but hardly a minute passes before

Slip is lying atop the bedsheets, asleep, breath reverberating like cat purrs.

Tagged key in hand, Slip stands undecided between the bed and the door, observing The Corpses in their bag as if they were tired children.

"I have to go out," Slip declares, but thinks it would be helpful if The Corpses could react in some way, any way, to this announcement, could respond by offering the subtlest inkling of their wishes or fears. Even if The Corpses could answer, *Do you want to come?* would not be a useful follow-up question, since The Corpses cannot be out in public. Perhaps Slip could ask, *What do you think will happen?* Even though dead bodies do not necessarily know more than living ones about the promises of the future, or lack thereof, Slip would appreciate their input, longs for support in this decision. A group consensus, a group preponderance—anything, really, other than self-doubt swinging like a pendulum in a world without friction. "No," Slip finally sighs. "I won't tell you why I'm going out. I'll explain everything when I get back."

Three blocks of darkened road have passed beneath the wheels of the trailer when Slip decides that The Corpses cannot be left alone in the motel room. Doubled locks can stand no ground against meddlesome hoteliers. Slip goes back, scoops the satchel from the desk with a resigned sigh, and leaves for a second time.

They drive the length of the downtown main street twice while Slip surveys the nightlife. The Corpses haven't said *What are you doing?* but it would be a reasonable question to ask, especially now that The Corpses are joining the outing, so Slip relents and answers preemptively.

"The clerk in the gas station was no help at all. Lac Lemot was hardly more beautiful than a landfill. We need to find a stranger who gives better advice, but we also need someone who won't remember us later. So we're going out to find a barfly."

Slip dismisses the sports bars as too loud, the extended-hour restaurants with liquor licenses as too subdued, the lounges as too charged, the dive bars as too empty, and the live music venues as over-crowded with standing patrons. By the number of bars alone, it is obvious how much more of a city this is than Euphoria, which is a relief to Slip, for cities offer anonymity. Finally, Slip chooses an establishment set in the middle of a line of row shops. They are, by appearance, the oldest buildings on the street—two-storeys built with red brick, commercial spaces on the bottom, residential apartments on top, a dozen windows blinking from a long, shared mansard roof.

Stepping inside the bar and noting the walls of wood and exposed brick, the plainly-dressed patrons at most but not all tables, the lack of theme or pretension, the mid-volume music and mid-level prices written in chalk above the cash register, Slip nods approvingly. It is the kind of bar where no one has any reason to be suspicious, no reason to avoid each other or to pay all that much attention to each other. Nevertheless, Slip maintains a one-handed grasp on the strap of the satchel.

"What can I get you tonight?" the bartender asks once Slip is settled a few seats down from the interior corner of the bar, farthest from the entrance and closest to the exit, between a pair of people in deep conversation on the right side, and a lone drinker on the left. It is a predictable question, but Slip is afraid of asking for the wrong thing, of being identifiable as an outsider. Countless bottles, some crystalline-clear, some in tints of amber, juniper, and cornflower, gleam like insect wings in the dim light. Slip's grip on the satchel tightens, though its weight is held by one abbreviated arm of the stool. On Slip's left side, the lone barmate holds out an empty shot glass to the bartender.

"Another, please."

"Sure thing." The bartender takes the glass while maintaining eye contact with Slip.

"What's popular?" Slip asks.

The bartender smiles impishly and walks away.

"You must not drink very often," says the barmate, watching a nature documentary playing out silently on the TV over the bar.

"I can't remember the last time I did," Slip admits, studying the barmate briefly. Grey-haired, just finished a drink, not craning at fellow customers as if seeking attention. Desperate people, Slip thinks, are too easy to make an impression on. It's preferable to find someone like this, who is neither friendly nor unfriendly.

"Why are you having one today?" the barmate asks.

"It's a special day," Slip replies.

"Happy birthday."

"Oh, it's not my birthday."

For the first time, the barmate turns to consider Slip.

"What's special about it then?"

"I guess you could say I'm on vacation."

"Very hedging," the barmate says, with a barely visible upward tilt of the lips.

"If you don't like it, it's on the house," the bartender says, as a tumbler of ice and orange fog materializes in front of Slip, though the bartender has already careened away to another part of the bar by the time Slip looks up. Slip lifts the glass and scrutinizes its contents dubiously. "What do you think this is?" Slip asks the barmate, who is fully grinning now.

"That's a pussyfoot."

"Sorry I don't think I heard you right."

"The cocktail's called a pussyfoot. It's what that bartender always gives someone who can't decide on a drink."

"You must come here often, to be so familiar with the bartender's habits."

"Now and again."

Slip lifts the glass hesitantly and prods the contents with a straw. "Is it safe?"

"Are you allergic to fruit, cream, or rum?"

"I don't think so."

"Then it's probably safe. Though whether you enjoy it or not…" As the barmate trails off, Slip takes an experimental gulp, shrugs, sets the tumbler back down.

"I don't have much to compare it to," Slip says.

"That's to your benefit."

"What are you drinking?"

"Brandy. A far better use of fruit than yours."

"Next time I'm in a bar I'll try that instead." Slip glances quickly at the satchel, which has not moved beneath the hand that grips it, then does another reconnaissance of the room. Beside them, a new pair of people has replaced the former. These two are laughing boisterously, touching each other's forearms, shoulders, knees. The situation is tolerable. "You must be a local if you come here regularly?"

"Correct."

"Maybe you can help me with something then."

"Does it involve lifting anything? I'm not as strong as I look." The barmate slaps a placid bicep.

"You actually don't look—" Slip stops, pivots. "You don't need to be strong. I just have a question you might be able to answer."

"Try me, then."

"Where is the most meaningful place you have ever been?"

"That's an odd question. Meaningful to whom?"

"To you, I suppose?"

"Like my parents' house—most meaningful to my development as a person? Or like the place I have the fondest memories of? Or?"

"Yes, I see why the question is a problem." Slip's once-protruding ice cubes have begun to melt, swelling the orange cocktail to a depth Slip feels capable of drowning in. "What about this: which place on Earth has moved you the most?"

"You want me to talk about how a fixed place, a single geographical location, has moved me. That's kind of funny."

"You're picking my words apart. You know what I mean, don't you?" It's a rhetorical question because Slip has already presumed the answer and is annoyed. Why does the barmate think this is a game?

"You want to hear about how I climbed a mountain and went into ecstasies over a double rainbow, or about how I fell to my knees before the sublime beauty of a painting. That sort of thing."

"Well, have you?"

"I've seen some nice sights, but none that made me faint. Sorry." The barmate, put off, perhaps, by having a casual night out weighed down by Slip's fumbling attempts at profundity, rotates away from Slip, and night settles back over the world.

"Can I get you anything?" The bartender's voice echoes in the void surrounding Slip.

"The cheque," Slip says. Under Slip's anxious index finger, a button on the satchel is as frictionless and smooth as wet ice.

CONSULTING THE PSYCHIC

"Where are we going?" Mal asks.

"Just a little further," Limn replies, refusing to really answer, because if Mal hears that they are going to talk to a psychic there will be an argument and they will still go anyway. Soon the flamingo pink and diner blue of the neon sign will give everything away anyhow, but then there will hardly be time for protest.

"The video store?" Mal says incredulously but Limn leads them past Utopia Video in dignified silence, stopping a few doors down. "Oh, you're joking." Mal sighs, eyeing the moon, stars, and palm beneath the rounded, sans serif typeface of a modified Century Gothic.

The door Limn opens is mahogany-dark, the windows beside it curtained with heavy shades, as if the future is a matter of great secrecy. They ascend a dimly-lit wooden staircase, past sage green wallpaper adorned with faded gold figures whose limbs are bent into motions of dance.

"Going to a psychic. Where did you even come up with that?"

Late at night, when Limn watches true crime shows alone, there are often commercials for telephone lines where you can pay by the minute to seek spiritual and astrological counsel. Those people are frauds,

Limn suspects, but the local psychics, who can say? Certainly not Limn, who has never actually visited one. Maybe the psychic will be able to tell Limn and Mal who those bones belonged to.

At the top of the stairs, they reach another closed door, empty of signage. Limn knocks three times, loudly enough to be assertive, quietly enough to be polite. There is silence. Then, the scrape of chair legs on the floor, footsteps, a voice inquiring, "Who's there?"

"You tell us," Mal snickers quietly, and receives a half-hearted elbow to the ribs from Limn.

"We're here for a reading," Limn answers, and the door cracks open.

The psychic scrutinizes the kids from top to toe, exhales loudly, relents.

"Fine, come in." The psychic's voice is flat, bored, as though cosmic forecasting, like banking or dentistry or any other profession, can become exhaustingly dull through repetition. The door swings wide and the kids take in the psychic for the first time, a short and broad silhouette in the scarcely-lit murk of a room whose purple walls are obscured by stacks of boxes that loom precariously over the small, round table draped with layers of twilight fabrics of variable length and weave. The psychic sits without ceremony and waits for the kids to do the same. "What kind of reading do you want?"

"The cheap kind," Mal says, earning another elbow below the ribs from Limn, who wishes that psychic shops came with menus like restaurants do.

"How much for a crystal ball reading?" Limn asks.

"Thirty."

"Dollars?" Mal yips. The psychic turns and stares impassively at Mal.

"What can you do for…" Limn counts loonies, then quarters, then dimes, then nickels. "Ten dollars?"

"I'll give you a two-card tarot reading."

"Deal."

"Shuffle," the psychic instructs, handing the deck to Limn, who accepts the cards and rearranges them slowly and tentatively, afraid to dog-ear their edges and disrupt whatever magic might possess them. The backs of the cards are a glossy black, filigreed with gold.

"For how long should I shuffle them?" Limn asks.

"Until you're done."

Limn goes on shuffling nervously, dovetailing the cards over and over, afraid to leave the job incomplete, until finally the psychic reaches across the table and takes back the deck. "What do you want to ask the cards?"

"Isn't that like, a leading question?" Mal asks. "Shouldn't you know, or shouldn't the cards know, what we need to be told without us having to say it?"

Silence stretches on for so long that Limn is sure no answer is forthcoming, but then the psychic says, dry and deliberate: "I'm a fortune teller, not a mind reader."

Mal, who sometimes enjoys being bested, guffaws appreciatively, and the tension of the room eases by a pound-force.

"We think…" Limn hesitates, then starts again. "There is someone who currently lives, I mean is staying, here, in Euphoria, or near here, and who is possibly missing, whose family or friends or whoever are probably worried. Because this person just looks lost, all the time. But we can't just go talk to this person, who is a stranger, right? A stranger won't talk to us. Won't confide in us about something that important.

Maybe doesn't even remember. In any case is very mistrustful. We can barely even get a good look at this person. But we don't want to call the police and cause any trouble. We just want a name, maybe a hint about whether we should look for family or friends to tell. Does that make sense?"

The psychic, whose eyes are closed, nods, then hands the deck to Limn. "Take two cards and put them face down on the table." Limn complies, and the psychic flips over the first card. "The Star. You are very close to where you need to be."

"Right now? Literally this minute we are very close to a particular clue? Or just like, in general we should continue with what we're doing to find out who this person is?" Limn asks.

"The cards haven't told me that."

"How does that—" Mal gestures at the card, where, posed against the velvet backdrop of a sidereal sky, a human figure pours water from a pitcher into the sea "—communicate to you that we are very close to where we need to be?"

The psychic shrugs. "It just does. Do you need to understand how sound waves work, do you need to memorize the circle of fifths, in order to sing?" It is the kids' turn to shrug. The psychic flips over the second card. "Hmm. The Falling Tower." The kids peer at the card, which depicts flames escaping through the windows of a stone belfry. "You say there is one person missing, but there are many people who are now lost."

"What does that mean?" Limn presses, anxious.

"You tell me," the psychic says. "I only convey what the cards want you to hear. They aren't concerned with whether the message makes sense to me, and neither am I."

LAST ROAD

Pacing the motel room, Slip assesses their progress while The Corpses observe the proceedings from the table.

"We haven't accomplished anything, and worse, I see no prospect of us accomplishing anything. We don't even know where we're going tomorrow morning. No one is any help. No one is ever any help. I'm alone even when I'm not alone. And you." Small is the skull that Slip lifts from the satchel. Such an insubstantial presence without the expressive heft of muscle, fat, skin, hair. Slip's impatience gives way to pathos. "What will I do with you, whom I have taken from your grave?

"I might as well tell you, since I'm sure you've long since figured it out, that the whole purpose of this road trip, the reason I've been driving you over all these landscapes, was that I thought I could find you the perfect final resting place. The most beautiful, or the most peaceful, or the most touching. I thought we would find somewhere nicer than those lonely woods. But it's like trying to pick the perfect wedding ring for a stranger. Impossible. I think it might have been wrong for me to ever move you at all. Just tell me: would I be doing the right thing now, to bring you back to the Unwood?"

Shadows shiver in the deep sockets of the skull, as light flickers in a living eye.

"Yes, I think so, too," Slip says. "There is only one road now, and it is the one that leads us back to Euphoria."

With a mind made even more certain by the illumination of morning, Slip herds The Corpses back into the trailer and sets them on a path heading south. "I need to find out what it is you want, which means that I need to find out who you are, and who you have been. Which means that we need to go back."

Two days later, on a balmy evening amid the blush of dusk, Slip and The Corpses drift through the orchards on the outskirts of Euphoria. It is late in the summer. Branches of cherry trees are barren; crab apple trees have begun to offer up their fruit. Cicadas, loudest of the world's 5,000,000 insects, have already been foretelling the coming frost for weeks. Through these signs, the season is reminding Slip that the time for endings is approaching.

They drive past the trailer park, stopping on the side of the road a few hundred metres from the forest. Slip shoulders the satchel and proceeds on foot. In the Unwood, the dry hollow of a dead tree becomes a temporary home for the bones. Bedding them down in fallen leaves, Slip swallows, uses the bottom of a cotton shirt to disappear fingerprints from the buttons and buckles of the satchel.

"There," Slip declares. "Now our relationship is invisible."

TRUE CRIME

Trying to come to terms with one's neighbour possibly being a murderer might reasonably lead to an intense interest in accounts of real-life violence. Or, at least, this proves to be the case for Limn, who has begun to hover on channels broadcasting melodramatic true crime reenactments by theatre school dropouts late at night; who now leafs through the newspaper seeking hints of sinister circumstances afoot in Euphoria that could explain why there are bones hidden in the trailer of someone who had never previously given offence; who wanders the non-fiction section of the library skimming synopses on the backs of books looking for a depiction of a comparable situation that might prove educational.

Limn's parent does not share this true crime fixation and so does not really understand why the tiny living room, where they always sit to watch TV together, is suddenly populated in the evenings by mobsters and con artists, scorned adulterers and serial killers. At first, Limn hid these burgeoning morbid fascinations, but has come to believe that the parent would benefit from being made to confront the prevalence of violence and be reassured of the real or feigned capacity of forensics to uncover and rectify such widespread harms. Limn thinks this will all be good preparation for the big reveal and continues to monitor the influence the macabre TV shows are having on the parent's worldview, while also trying to determine the opportune moment to throw open the curtains on their neighbour's misdeeds.

After the breakfast table incident, there were several further false starts, before Limn finally settles on an evening when the parent has just switched back to day shifts and is, if not relaxed, then somewhat suggestible thanks to the combined effects of alcohol and exhaustion. There is, furthermore and fortuitously, a story on TV about a remarkably harmless-looking individual whose root cellar had been searched, after death, by the unfortunate and unwitting estate trustees, and had been found to contain a full 16 skeletons, later identified as the remains of various missing persons, mostly hitchhikers and other vagrants from the surrounding region, some of whom had been lost for decades. It was a shocking discovery for the neighbours, many of whom still spoke as if wondering whether their own lives had ever been in danger. *It was never anyone from our street, you know,* one person being interviewed said. *The victims were people coming down the highway,* the person's spouse added.

Limn keeps offering to get the parent another beer, and is repeatedly rebuffed, and so finally stops asking, but instead goes to the refrigerator during a commercial break, returning to the couch with a can of grape soda and a beer, silently replacing the parent's old bottle with the fresh one. "It really makes you wonder about the people around you," Limn says when the segment ends.

"You can't trust anyone," the parent agrees. "That's why I stay single." Limn expects laughter, but none follows.

"You know, I saw something strange in the trailer park a few days back," Limn starts.

"They're all fucking oddballs around here. Too much time on their hands, not enough expensive shit like travel and antiques to waste it on."

"Right, yeah. But this was extra strange. It was that neighbour who used to live at 7A, the one whose trailer's been gone for a while."

"The one who never speaks? Slip, I think?"

"Oh, that's probably it. I thought it was Skip or something." Limn pauses, recovers the point. "I mean, even just the fact that Slip left is a bit weird, isn't it?"

"Could be taking a trip."

"The person who's like 90 years old and has never taken a trip since I was big enough to walk, is off on vacation?"

"Probably only 80 years old."

"There's more though. A couple of weeks before the move-out, I saw something suspicious in the trailer."

"What?" the parent straightens abruptly and stares pointedly at Limn. "Why would you be in that trailer?"

"I wasn't, I was just, you know."

"Just what?"

"Looking in the windows."

"Why are you going around looking in strangers' windows? Are you trying to get into trouble?"

"Is someone we've lived a 100 feet away from since I was born really a stranger?"

"Yes, really and truly."

"This is beside the point."

"No, this is definitely exactly my point."

"Don't you want to know what I saw?"

"Fine."

"Bones. Like a whole skeleton's worth, at least. They filled a bag. It was creepy."

"Did you ever think that maybe they were animal bones from a hunt? Hell, they could've been theatre props. Halloween decorations. A taxidermy project. Any goddamn thing. But you assumed, what? That we're living shoulder to shoulder with some kind of homicidal octogenarian?"

"I'm pretty sure they were human and pretty sure they were real—"

"Pretty sure, were you doc?"

"I think it's a big coincidence that our neighbour is discovered to be in possession of human bones and then uproots and leaves town soon after."

"*In possession of.* You are watching way too many of those crime docs lately. Can't you be a normal teenager and stick to sitcoms or something?"

"You *just* said no one can be trusted."

"I meant don't give anyone the PIN for your credit card. Lock your door when you're away from home. That kind of thing."

"I don't have a credit card."

"You know what I mean."

An hour ago, Limn bet against the parent's capacity for sustained argument. Now Limn senses that it is about to be a losing gamble unless there is a turn of circumstance in the homestretch. "I hear what you're saying," Limn says calmly. "And I know the chances are low that I'm right. *But what if I am?*"

"They're not our bones, so it's someone else's problem."

"I'm not saying I want to become a vigilante out for revenge on behalf of the dead. I'm just saying maybe it would be a good idea to tell someone who can look into it. Someone whose job it is to do that kind of thing."

"The police will probably think you're pranking them."

"I could tell park management." *Again.*

"The manager will definitely think we're busybodies. And what could be done anyway? Someone gonna sift the dirt of lot 7A for bone fragments?"

"Eventually rent will come due. The manager might call the police."

The parent laughed heartily.

"It'll get put on our neighbour's credit report, same as happens to everyone else, and that'll be that."

"You're wrong," Limn mutters inaudibly, huffing off to bed.

GOTHIC REVIVAL

"I have to bury you," Culver, who is driving, says.

There is no reply from the passenger seat.

"I cannot carry you with me to the end. I would have, you know, but you made it impossible."

Culver's eyes flick in repetitive succession, from windshield, to hood, to asphalt, to shoulder, monitoring a progression. Raindrops, soft as light snow, stipple the windshield, texturing the garnet hood of the car. They gloss the asphalt, darkening the dusty shoulder by degrees. Nothing is soaked yet—what will Culver do if the ground becomes too wet, the sand too heavy to lift? It is still a half hour to the lake Culver has in mind, a small, desolate one a little ways past Lac Lemot's largest beach, still far enough away that the rain could become a real problem.

Windshield, hood, asphalt, shoulder. A fluid motion, just like all the times that Culver surveyed Blue top to toe. Eyes, shoulder, hands, ankles. Past and present begin to overlap. Culver sees Blue's familiar body superimposed on the road ahead.

"We could have done this together, but you wanted to do it alone, do it your own way, as you always have. Do you remember the first time we slept together? It was at your apartment, in your bed. Do you remember when we bought the house? It was the architectural style you chose. You were so in love with Cape Cods. You said they were the only kind of house that could feel like home. Ironic, wasn't it? You didn't grow up in a house like that, grew up in the opposite, in fact—a gaudy Second Empire, with its tower and balcony and wrought iron gallery, a place for luxurious people to fret and languish. When I longed for a Gothic Revival you dismissed the idea, saying they were too complicated and intimidating, the blood-red brick too harsh, spider-silk vergeboards too shivery and slight. Truthfully, I think that style reminded you a little too much of your parents and the elaborate trap they made you live in. We did go to see a Gothic Revival, of course, just so you could placate me, and as we left you said, *How could anyone ever feel settled there?* Yes, those were your exact words.

"I keep asking you if you remember this, remember that, but I don't think you do. Since the beginning I have been the hippocampus, the container of our memories—I wrote them down if I had to, constructed calendars of our hours. You didn't. You preferred to reimagine our history, building and rebuilding to suit your capricious moods. I wouldn't indulge that and you resented me for it. You hated the way I would bring out my papers mid-argument just to show you the record of what really happened. *You wrote it down wrong,* you'd say, when your emotions disagreed with my archive. Jealous, I think, of the constancy of my purpose, a feat you yourself could never quite achieve. You stayed with me for a long time, though, I'll grant you that. Longer than I expected. When you left, it was not in the manner I predicted. But you did leave."

Culver reaches the beach parking lot within minutes of the projected arrival time, noting this fact with satisfaction. "3:00 p.m.," Culver says. "Exactly as I promised." The clock reads 3:03 p.m.

The beach is empty of human guests. Toeing the sand, Culver finds that there is only a scant dampness on the surface, beneath which the ground is dry and yields easily to the press of a shovel. "Everything falls into place as it's supposed to," Culver says. "Except you, usually. This time, for once, you will go where I put you."

Deeper and deeper grows the hole, Culver worrying foot by foot that it will be too shallow, particularly given that a beach is hardly an ideal location for a burial even under the best of circumstances. "You deserve this, my dear," Culver says, lowering a sack into the cache. Black fabric huddles in the hole like a wounded mammal, until it is covered over completely with sand. "Interred on the ground where we were married."

Skimming the shoreline one final time for visitors, Culver meets the eye of a bird watching the proceedings from a nearby tree. Crow-like but streaked with white, the bird's name only comes to Culver after a moment's reflection: magpie.

CONFLUX

Without The Corpses, Slip is at a loss for who to talk to when alone in the trailer, especially at night. The clock has a face but no expression; the toaster has an arm but its panels are mirrors; shoes have soles but their tongues are tied. None of them offer reprieve from the feeling that one is only ever talking to oneself.

Slip sits at the table cracking saltines into craggy shards and chewing them carefully. Into the empty space of this seemingly interminable seclusion, a knock on the door comes stumbling like an accident.

Slips waits stiffly for a voice to follow, but none is forthcoming. Tawny lamplight and a trickle of music escaping through the thin panes of the windows will have already disclosed Slip's presence in the trailer to anyone outside—there can be no hiding that now. If only the visitor would reciprocate and reveal something, Slip might engage.

Another knock on the door, though tentative rather than demanding, makes it nevertheless evident that, accident or not, this matter will have to be handled. Slip goes to a window, nudges the curtain an eyeball-width to the side, and peers out at the visitor.

This is a shock: there are two visitors. One lanky and equine, the other closer to the ground but with a mass of hair that leaps like wildfire in the slight breeze. It is difficult to discern more than that in the muddy dark of the evening. The two are familiar to Slip, who thinks they might be teenagers from the park, though it is hard to be sure.

"Who's there?" Slip calls quaveringly from behind the curtain. Confused, the visitors crane to trace the source of the voice.

"I don't think we know each other," the rangy one says in the window's general direction. "We live here in the park, too, and we don't want any trouble, we'd just like to talk to you."

"About what?" Slip asks. The two visitors bend their heads together in conference.

"We'd rather not say it out in the open." It is the smaller one who speaks.

"Have it your way." Slip lets the curtain go and walks with great, deliberate, stomping steps back to the table.

"You'd also probably rather we don't say it out in the open," one of them adds loudly and pointedly.

Slip returns to the door, answers with a defensive hiss, "Oh really."

"It's about the…you know."

The Corpses, Slip surmises. What else could it be? Dread spreads like pain through Slip's limbs.

Cracking open the door lets loose a sliver of light. "No, I don't know," Slip says. "Whisper it to me if it's such a big secret." The door is only open wide enough that Slip can hear more clearly, but still cannot see the guests.

"Bones," one of them says.

"Bones?" Slip feigns innocence. "What bones?"

"Human, I think," the other of them says. "I saw them in your trailer."

"There are no bones in my trailer." Slip snaps the door shut with a smirk, secure in the conviction that all the best lies are true.

FALTER

Security proves unsustainable, a circumstantial advantage narrowly gained. Three days after the kids' visit, Slip paces the trailer on tender legs, a tremulous glass of bracing pineapple juice in hand, mortally afraid of being tailed in the future by the kids, who might thereby discover the hitherto secluded hinterland of the Unwood with its obvious agglomeration of human remains. Worse—what if they have already done this, their recent efforts at contact just the first steps in an extortion plan? What they might expect to obtain from someone as under-resourced as Slip is a matter of doubt, but it is not for the childless to fathom the minds of the young. There is only one way through this. Tomorrow, Slip must go at will to talk to the kids.

QUODLIBET

"I did something you're not going to like," Fir says.

"How do you know that?" Fain says. "Am I so judgmental? So predictable?"

"You're a person of ordinary qualms."

"That sounds like an insult."

"I just mean that you're normal."

"Ouch."

"You have a conventionally-calibrated moral compass?"

"Ethical *atrocities* have been justified by ordinariness, normalcy, and convention," Fain points out.

"I followed some kids home and surveilled one of them for a few hours," Fir admits in one quick rush of words.

"You're right, I don't like that. How about you tell me why before I tell you off?" Above Fir and Fain's heads, a revolving disco ball tosses sequins of light that fall scattershot on the glossy wood floor. "But take your turn first, we look weird just standing here."

Fir chooses the nearest specimen, shelled with hot pink coverstock, from the ball return and launches it like a bottle rocket down the lane.

"I think I saw sparks fly," Fain says.

"I'm a fast throw," Fir agrees, as they watch the ball zing into the electric blue gutter. "But not very accurate."

Bowling had been Fain's idea, proffered because Fir was anxious to get out of the house and even more anxious about being overheard. It has proven to be a sound suggestion. Dance hits, all a decade or more out of date, blare exuberantly through staticky speakers. Herds of teenagers, families, seniors overwhelm the alley, making a rat's nest of motion and noise. A menagerie of neon adorns the walls with irrelevance: tropical fish with fanning tails, verdant trees of indiscernible species, a single horse. Anyone trying to pay attention to Fir and Fain will be confronted by such an excess of stimuli that it might as well be a wall protecting them from prying eyes and prurient ears.

"Two teenagers came into the video store a few nights ago," Fir starts.

"Are they teenagers you know?"

"I was sure I'd seen them in the store before, but I didn't have the vaguest idea of what their names were. I do now though. Limn and Malapert."

"Odd names. How old are they?"

"With every year that passes, I become less and less capable of guessing anyone's age. Does that happen to you?"

"Yeah. I think it's because the older you are, the more times you've guessed someone's age wrong, and when you realize how often you're wrong, it becomes increasingly obvious how vague and variable the body's signs of aging really are. Probably as a child you were even worse at guessing people's ages, but you got corrected on it less often, so you didn't notice how bad you were at it."

"Probably. In any case, I'd say these kids were likely high-schoolers, 16 maybe? The two of them came in together when the shop was empty."

"When is the shop *not* empty?"

"You're so fixated on that. We get busy sometimes, I swear. But back to my story; the shop was empty so I could hear everything they were saying and they talked about having seen a body in a neighbour's trailer."

"A body! A whole body?"

"A skeleton or whatever. I don't remember how they worded it exactly."

"Okay."

"They had to give me the postal code for the trailer park when they checked out, of course, so that much I had solved. The problem was that they didn't mention which trailer the bones were in, or who lived there."

"And you didn't want to ask them because…"

"That would've been creepy. *Sorry, I couldn't help overhearing your entire conversation…*"

"So you followed them home, which is much less terrifying, obviously."

"I followed *one* of them home. The taller one, Limn. Don't worry, I kept my distance, I wasn't noticed."

"Are you sure?"

"Very sure. If you thought you were being followed, would you go sit by a pool alone for hours? Because that's what the kid I was following did."

"I guess I wouldn't. So did you find out where the body was hidden?"

"No. That's the current problem. I can't follow these kids around forever, hoping they lead me to the body."

"I'm glad you've come to realize that."

"Do you think I should go talk to them?" Fir picks up another ball, butterscotch-swirled as the bands of Jupiter.

"No, they're children. I think you should leave them alone."

"What kind of morbid kids go about looking for dead bodies anyhow?"

"You don't remember childhood very well, do you?"

"I remember some parts of it with improbable clarity."

"Maybe the kid didn't even actually see a body, but was just talking big to sound tough, or interesting. And even if it was an actual dead body, it might not be the dead body you're looking for. It's high-risk and a long shot. Just leave it alone. Wait to see if the situation develops. It's not like someone is holding your friend hostage and you have to act immediately."

"I respect your opinion very much, but I have to ask: what's the harm in following those kids around? You know I'm not going to hurt them. The whole point would be to get the information and then leave the kids out of it as quickly as possible."

"Excuse me," an unfamiliar voice interrupts them. Fir startles, colliding with Fain's shoulder. "Sorry."

"Sorry!" Fir parrots to no one specifically.

"I need that ball." The bowler's face is mostly obscured by a long fringe of bleached hair and a wealth of silver piercings.

"The ball in my hand?" Fir asks, nonplussed.

"It's the only ball in the whole place with the perfect weight block. I use it every time I bowl. Every Tuesday."

"You can have it," Fir says, handing it over and waiting until the intruder has diffused into the crowd. "Can you imagine the nerve to just go up to a complete stranger and ask—"

"For what you want?" Fain supplies.

"Don't make this about that."

"To answer your question more directly: the harm is that you will frighten the children. Or their parents. You'll get yourself in trouble because no one will believe you when you explain why you're following them around. Your sense of personal boundaries will begin to dissolve and next you'll do something more invasive."

"I just want to find someone I—care about. Who's *missing.*"

"A noble objective but it doesn't give you the right to use other people however you like. Now come on," Fain says, gesturing toward the scoreboard and then prodding Fir toward the exit door, "Let's get out of here before you lose for real."

They return their shoes and walk out of the building past a small mass of smokers casting clouds overhead.

Once they are nearly across the parking lot, beyond the earshot of the milling crowd, Fir looks up, demands of the stars, remote and obscure, "What am I supposed to do?"

"You need to wait," Fain answers.

"Wait for what?"

"Wait for something to happen."

"I've spent my entire life in Euphoria waiting for something to happen."

"There will be more opportune moments than this, I'm sure of it. The kids might come back to the store—a place you're obligated to be, so there can be no question of you having followed them— and you can gently ask about the conversation you overheard last time. The risk in that case shouldn't be *too* high."

"Too high for what? What precisely is the threshold in this scenario? This sounds like a bad idea."

"Well, we ran out of good ideas months ago," Fain says casually and Fir makes an inscrutable sound that might be a sigh or a curse. "The police will get involved and identify the body they found and you won't have to do anything."

"Why is everything always up to someone else?"

"I can't think of anything more helpful to tell you. And it's almost midnight. I'm going home."

Neither Fir nor Fain bothers to offer the other a goodnight wish, perhaps because the night is nearly over and there is little chance of it becoming good. Fir, watching the departing shape of Fain become more and more blurred until it is absorbed completely by the dark, is tired of people disappearing.

COMPLOT

Pool noodles in radiant shades of watermelon, lime, and mango populate the surface of the water like sprinkles on a sheet cake, between which a far smaller number of children's neutral-toned heads bob like errant crumbs. On deck chairs draped with towels, Limn and Mal are lounging in their sunglasses and sopping bathing suits, letting their wet hides dry in the sun.

"Nice day," Slip says mildly after sitting for several minutes unnoticed in a nearby chair. The kids bolt upright with alarm.

"Nice day," Mal parrots, lifting sunglasses and nodding excessively.

"Definitely," Limn chimes, slightly out of breath.

"It's going to rain later, though," Mal says.

"Oh?" Turning, Slip assesses Mal. "Watched the weather report this morning, did we?" The 'we' is a nice touch, establishing collectivity.

"No." It's Limn who answers. "There's a smell before rain, apparently. Mal can always tell when it's coming."

"I thought it was a smell after rain," says Slip. "What's that word? Not petrification."

"Petrichor," Mal eagerly corrects. "That's the part everybody knows. It occurs when rain hits the ground. Most people don't realize it can even show up before the storm reaches you. If you're downwind of wherever the storm starts, the scent will blow right in ahead of the clouds. But I'm not talking about petrichor. I can smell rain before it even exists, while the water is still waiting to condense into a cloud."

"Allegedly," Limn adds.

"Isn't that something," Slip says. "I've never heard that one before."

The kids are trying to play it cool, politely evading the very subject they want to broach, in the hope of easing everyone into a conversational mode that will prompt Slip to disclose some detail of interest. It has been a long time since Slip so readily held anyone's attention, and there is a temptation to make a long and digressive address, to watch the listeners' faces as they try to parse the speech for subtext, for some hint of what they actually want to know.

"Would you two mind helping me with something?" Slip asks. "I need to move some furniture in my trailer and these old bones won't carry much anymore." Both kids pitch further forward in their chairs.

"We can help," Limn rushes to say, too desperate for answers to be nervous. The kids leap from their seats in synchrony.

"Excellent." With exaggeratedly feeble steps to ensure that no one will question the pretext that has been spun, Slip leads the covey to the trailer, teenagers crowding behind.

"I need help with the trunk in the living room," Slip says once they enter the trailer, gesturing the kids in the direction of the couch, then carefully shuts the door and checks that the windows are closed so they cannot be overheard. "Sit down. Can I get you some water? Juice?" With a shake of the head, Limn declines.

"Do you have whiskey?" Mal asks.

"No." Slip remains standing in the kitchenette, preferring not to sit down, though unsure of how long that can last. "I don't drink."

"Oh, okay. Nothing for me then." Leaning back on the couch, Mal glances casually around the trailer, as if trying to avoid taking on the look of a crestfallen would-be underager who was really angling for alcohol, putting on, instead, the disaffected airs of an adult who is satisfied in having a stocked liquor cabinet waiting at home. Slip reads this as a kind of power play.

"As I'm sure you've figured out," Slip says, "I did not bring you here to move furniture."

"We did figure," Mal replies.

"I have a few questions for you first. Then I will tell you about the bones." For Slip right now, words are shaky rocks making a footpath through a treacherous river—they are to be navigated deftly and precisely in this sort of conversation. Conservative use of contractions. No informality except in the form of carefully selected, casual affectation. Slip is being overly conscious of linguistic rigour while speaking, in a way the kids don't seem to be, though Limn is noticeably taciturn.

"Ask away," Mal says.

Slip pockets a nervous hand. "Which of you saw the bones?"

"Me." Eyes lowered, Limn raises a hand, as if they are in a classroom.

"And what exactly did you see?" Slip asks.

"Oh no," Mal interjects, standing up. "You want to know what we saw so you can tailor your story to fit. We're not doing that."

"Fine," Slip replies. "Then get out of my trailer." As Slip and Mal stand across from each other, eyes locked in a challenging stare, it occurs to Slip for the first time that they are about the same height.

"I didn't see much." Limn touches the wrist of Mal, who grudgingly sits. "Just some bones in a kind of backpack thing. They looked human, or human-sized at least, so I got suspicious."

"Have you told anyone about this?" Slip asks.

"Yeah, but they didn't believe me."

"Did you tell the cops?"

"No."

"Who then?"

"My parent, and the park manager."

"What did they say?"

"Told me to mind my own business."

"You'd be wise to," Slip watches Limn hunch even further inward. "In the future."

"Your turn," Mal says.

Legs aching, Slip remains upright only with concerted effort, noticing—with the flicker of a small epiphany that will only come to full flame sometime later when all thoughts at last converge upon that single point—how unfair and irrational it seems that people so often try to read truth through the cipher of the body. Tremors in the hand are taken to signify a lie, the literality of shifting feet refigured into a shiftiness of character. As if frailty were an infection that could spread from limbs to mind to morals. Momentarily edified by anger, Slip remains standing and proceeds. "First of all, I did not kill anyone, if that's what you've been thinking. They are human bones, but I found them in the forest. I don't know whose they are and I don't know how they got there."

"Where are they now?" Limn asks.

"Back in the forest, where I found them." That apparent clarification—*where I found them*—is actually, ironically, an obfuscation, smoothly gliding straight past the road trip, which would be too difficult to innocently explain. Slip is well aware of the deceitful feat and even rather pleased by it.

"So you brought them from the forest to the trailer and then back to the forest." Limn sounds unimpressed. "Why?"

This makes Slip laugh. "Why? *You're* asking me why I returned them to the forest?" More laughter from Slip, who stands slowly and begins to shuffle deliberately toward the kids. "I'll tell you why." Step. "Nosey parkers." Step. "Finks and buttinskies." Step. "Prattlers and tattlers and fussbudgets and flibbertigibbets." Slip leans down, face within a foot of the kids' faces. "People. Like. You."

"No," Limn whispers. "I mean, why'd you take them out of the forest in the first place?"

Straightening up, Slip considers the kids for a moment and then returns to the kitchenette. "I didn't want anything bad to happen to them."

"They're dead. How much worse can it get?" Limn asks.

"They could be separated. They could be desecrated," Slip replies. "Same reason normal people put their dead family members in cemeteries instead of just tossing them by the roadside."

"Actually, we do that because it's the law," Limn says pedantically.

"Really?" Slip scoffs. "That's extremely disappointing."

"If you took us to see the bones, we could help you look for clues," Mal offers.

"Identity documents, phones, that sort of thing," Limn adds.

"We could report it to the police for you so you don't even have to get involved and they won't suspect you."

"I don't trust you enough for that," Slip says. "And even if I did, I am not taking two *children* to gawk at dead bodies."

"I'm 15," Limn says. "I'm not a child."

"And I'm 16," Mal adds. "I can drive."

"You can drive with supervision." Removed from the harsh light of interrogation now, Slip sits down.

"Wait a minute," Limn says. "Did you say *dead bodies?*"

"What?" Slip is confused.

"A minute ago you said you didn't want to take *two children* to look at *dead bodies."* No longer shyly evasive, Limn gazes levelly at Slip while quoting.

"Oh wow, you're right!" Mal flicks an admiring glance at Limn, before turning haughtily to Slip. "How many dead bodies are there?"

Being long past youth and having never raised children, Slip feels suddenly and unprecedentedly bereft of some crucial awareness of their habits, which might explain why the exchange at hand is not going particularly smoothly. *My mistake was calling them children. Children do not like to be called what they are.* Slip tucks away this observation for future conversations that have not already been damaged beyond recognition.

"I don't know how many bodies there are." Surely, Slip thinks, this frank admission will counteract the earlier, inadvertent tone of condescension.

"What do you mean you don't know?" Limn asks.

"How can you not know something like that?" Mal choruses. They both stare like cops and Slip recognizes that control of the discussion has been completely lost, if it was ever possessed at all.

"Have either of you found human remains in the wild before?" Slip asks. The kids shake their heads. "That's good." Slip pauses. "When an animal dies—human or otherwise—the forest does not just leave it alone. There's a whole ceremony. Predators and scavengers come one by one and strip the flesh from the body. They make use of everything; even what's too small to see is eaten clean away by insects and bacteria and turned to loam for plants. All that's left, for a while longer at least, is the skeleton. But without ligaments to hold it together, the skeleton is just pieces of bone that get scattered by animals, wind, water. Do you know what a pile of bones looks like?" The kids shake their heads again. "Not much. I didn't even know I'd found human bones until I saw the skull. The rest? Could've been deer bones, could've been dog bones."

"Once you assembled them, you'd be able to tell," Limn says.

"What do you think bones are? You think they're like those toy kit cars with tiny pieces you click into place until you have a full model? No. They're just a bunch of different-sized bits that don't look like anything much."

"Well how many skulls did you find?" Mal asks.

"Just one."

"Isn't that your answer then?" Mal retorts.

"Maybe there was another skull but it was dragged away by a hungry animal," Limn suggests.

"Exactly," Slip says.

"Why didn't you tell the police?" Limn asks.

"Why didn't you?" Slip returns.

"Thought they wouldn't believe me."

"That's what I thought as well."

"What's there to believe?" Mal asks. *I found some bones, here they are.*

"*I found some bones, but I didn't kill anyone,*" Slip rejoins.

"People find bones all the time," Limn says. "Normal people. Not even murderers."

"Innocent people become suspects all the time, too," Slip admonishes.

"Wait a minute," Mal says. "I can understand why you might not tell the police. But why are you telling *us?*"

"You're the firebrand of the group, are you?" Slip directs the question at Mal.

"Why do you say that?" Mal frowns.

"It's easy to suss out a troublemaker—it's whoever is asking all the toughest questions," Slip replies.

"We switch, actually," Limn says. "Depending on the circumstance."

"Yeah, like if I try to suggest we go to a party for once, it's that one," Mal points at Limn, "who won't shut up."

"In which case I'm trying to keep us *out* of trouble," Limn says. The kids face one another.

"But that's just between us." Mal says it as if noticing for the first time. "You're always quiet when someone else is around." Limn just shrugs.

"Anyways," Limn says, turning back to Slip. "We look out for each other. That's all."

"Yeah," Mal agrees. "Which reminds me: are you going to answer my question?"

"Right, of course, you want to know why I've brought you here, why I'm telling you these things." Slip sighs. "I wasn't lying before when I said I need your help. And you weren't wrong when you assumed I want to know who those bones used to belong to."

BLUE LANGUAGE

It is the rat who finds the letter. That crumpled paper, still damp in its creases and darkened with blood and yellowed with stomach acid, tucked alone into a plastic bag in the landfill. Hungry paws parse the folded layers until they all lie open.

I did not expect to be standing in my kitchen when I was told how and when my life would end. Why there? I still cannot say. Maybe it was the filthy plates strewn, not even stacked, across the counter, sulfurous skins of fried egg clinging to their rims, or the lavic crusts of hot sauce stuck between the tines of the forks. Maybe it was the homunculus—fashioned from our fallen hair, shed skin cells, and the exoskeletons of insects—who lived hidden behind the fridge. Maybe it was because we hadn't made love that morning, or yesterday, or even on any day in recent memory, ever since our baby wriggled like a fish through our fingers. I could almost understand how the slick viscera and fuzzy scuzz of life might leave a person willing to hand it all over to the deviceful scavengers of death.

Or maybe it was just gravity and passing time. The same forces at work when a cracked tree branch collapses. When a trickle of water flowing to the lowest point guts rock as if it were the delicate underbelly of a wading bird.

Then again maybe there was no reason, not even one as simple as physics or passing hours. Did I want there to be? If there was a reason, that would imply intelligibility, or worse, a justified order underlying being and event. The lurid trajectory of my death warrants no such flattery as that. And if I believe there was a cause that produced this effect, then I must ask myself whether I contributed to that cause, whether I had an unintentional hand in manifesting my own calamity. I would have to ask, too, what you were to me, Culver. Some kind of demiurge fashioning our shared reality? These are rabbit holes for dust bunnies— I won't go down.

I didn't and I don't and I'll never know what it was that morning that made you face me and say, there really is no joy in living, is there? I said, of course there is, and you said, there are moments of joy, yes, but what use are they? Marbles to hold back a flood when we need mountains made of sand. I said, what flood? And I regretted it for I had heard you crying often enough through the weight of doors over the years, and it only grew worse after we lost the baby.

You said, please understand, Blue, I've never loved anyone more than you. No one, not even myself. Especially not myself. You're the most splendid thing in all the world in all my life and we have done our best to be devoted to each other, haven't we? I said, yes. I think so. And you asked, but are you happy? Are you glad to be alive? Or do you wake every day dreading the repetition of tiresome routines? Worse—do you wake up feeling nothing at all? Your life just a series of rituals you maintain because your muscles remember when you do not. And even when our skins should be sliding over one another like sheets of silk, instead we are bells clanging inharmonic. But this is it, the best of life, the best of love. I can't go on watching all these things that meant so much to us become more and more trivial.

I know you feel the same. And if we don't make each other happy, then who ever will? Who ever can?

I said, we can fix this. You said, we haven't done anything wrong. We have been faithful and patient, we have been the most beautiful versions of ourselves, nurtured our lives within one another and without one another, and it is never enough. Well honey, I'm tired. I can't just go on trying forever.

It's not forever, I said. Someday we'll be dead.

And you said, death! Yes, isn't that what we've been waiting for? Let's not wait. Let's not allow life to have its way with us as if we were rats in its paws. I want to die in your arms. I want to die before it all keeps getting worse. Before we lose what's left of our youth, before we lose the last of our jouissance, before we lose another child, or three, or ten. We can disappear from this world together. A dreadful and impeccable ending that cannot be a failure because it's precisely what we intend. Beloved, what do you say?

I could not say anything—startled, of course, but also too miserable to speak. Had I been crestfallen before you mentioned it? I could no longer recall, which meant I could no longer disagree. Life is tiresome, love inevitably tepid, a situation we endure two by two in the ark of the ache so it follows that we would leave by an arc as well. Arc of the drama, arc of a falling star, electric arc that marks a luminous line from one body to the other. There was nothing for me to say. My empty mouth gaped before you and you tucked words into it like stones. I was dead before anything could kill me.

How? I asked, at last. We are gentle, sensitive people. Murder, suicide, these are brutal. Megaliths for mayflies. Not violence, you said, never violence. We only need to go to the Unwood and let it take us. You believe the old folk tales then? I asked. If I'm wrong, you said, we'll walk home.

I wanted to leave a note before we went. Why, you said, who will look for us? Maybe that was true, but I was less afraid of being lost than I was of being misunderstood. They might accuse us of torrid affairs and call our deaths crimes of passion, or suspect us of embezzlement and label us victims of a suicide pact enacted as an escape hatch. As if we were anachronisms, remnants of the dark ages. Cast us extraordinary and assess our catastrophes improbable. Ours a predestination they could expect never to share.

How would we compose the note? you scoffed. By consensus? Futures unwound before me, wormy skeins of wool: we both write the note, neither of us approve of what it says; one of us writes the note, it is no longer representative; we both write separate notes, now we are each on lonely trajectories that only happened to collide. I don't think we should leave a note, you said. We mustn't let people suppose that our deaths were meant to send a message to them.

I resented the way you took charge of our mortality, had to keep reminding myself that most of us do not get to preselect the details of our deaths, so it was no true loss to me. And really, if you trace the genealogy of the event, it originated in me anyhow. We were in the dim corner of a bar, the sort of place in which secrets crawl out from the crevices where they hide. Floorboards, folds of skin. We had only been on a few dates, we barely knew one another, and there I was talking about how I wanted to die. You were already in love with me, mooncalving, spilling affection all over the floor the way other people were tipping their beer. I didn't have to ask for anything because you had already spread your world like cloth beneath my feet and I accepted it: took the phone calls, the letters, the cufflinks with opalescent eyes. How are you? you asked. Your hourly question. Often you didn't need to ask—my face has always betrayed me to any observer as keen as you—but you asked regardless. I said, well

I am having a very nice time with you, rather exquisite really, unbearable even.

You did not understand. You had never thought about dying, except as an abstraction, as an event that happened to someone else. I asked, have you ever had a precise slice in your skin, just one small, sublime rift? Your blood rushes through it as if that opening were a holy portal, as if that was the ultimate vein through which your current was meant to flow. Red and white blood cells form a river of jewels gushing from your cut and the pain is clear as ice, tart as lemons, bright as sunlight. A rupture so flawless that you are in awe of it.

Excising a lemon wedge from a glass dish on the table, you placed it, flesh and rind, into your mouth and swallowed it whole. As if you were a common sea snake. Only after did I see that you were eating the lemon but envenoming me through your version of sympathetic enchantment. It wasn't real magic, just one of those sublunary spells through which we all must pass in some form or another.

I was the second lover but I would be the first corpse. You said that was how it had to be. I would walk before you into the Unwood and let it have me, for I was a coward, emptied of courage, and if you entered first I would turn tail and run. There was no such lacuna in you. No gaps in the manuscript, no minute cavities in the bone. Your absence of lack approached inhumanity. You were a colossus, swelled by a surfeit of romantic fanaticism. That is how you had always been: passionate, excessive, stubbornly unreasonable. A compelling trifecta but, in this instance, I was not sufficiently convinced. You would have to goad me to the last.

It's not as if I have ever been the one to be relied upon. You have always been the mapmaker, the adjudicator, the driver. There was one thing, though, that I chose.

Before we do this, I said, we must each be allowed one indulgence. What does that mean? you asked querulously. It means that we will permit each other one luxury, I said. Something we would not ordinarily accept for ourselves, or each other. You mean an indiscretion, you said, and your eyes flashed with wounded anger. We have been so good, I said. Just once let us try something entirely different. That is all I ask, and then we can proceed exactly as we have agreed.

Though you have often been possessive and judgmental, you have also as often been generous. You have given me all and expected as much in return. As I predicted, you capitulated to my request. Traded your concession for mine.

For a few weeks, I existed without you, nestled in the soft crevice of my past. But a person cannot live in reverse. I returned to you, ready for dissolution.

Remember how we were both vegetarian when we met? I asked one night as I watched you spear salmon fillet with your fork, and I prodded a wax bean with mine. You refused meat for ethical reasons, you said. And you were just terrified of dead bodies, I finished. We both laughed. I thought our plan popped like a balloon then, too thin-skinned to hold its own absurdity.

Did you know, you said to me once, after we had made our arrangement, that you can drink yourself to death with too much water? It's so sweet and clear that it will wash the salt from your veins, until you are so pure that your brain swells and you perish. That's what happiness is like.

Are you having second thoughts about our plan? I asked you another night as we sat, preparing for sleep. Why are you asking me that? you said in return, folding your horn-rimmed glasses and setting them on the bedside table. Is it because you're having second thoughts? No, I said, pausing to take a sip from my water glass, I'm just checking. Forgive me for thinking so, you said, I'm sure you can see how it looks from where I'm sitting. Of course, I replied, but try not to get so excitable over a simple question. Communication is essential in a situation like this. You can't let yourself get carried away by your suspicions. I never get carried away, you replied. You do often think you're right and won't hear otherwise, though, I said. Only when I am right, you added. Your certainty, I said, is the part of you I understand least of all. And your uncertainty is the part of you I like least of all, you rejoined.

Days later, I stopped in the middle of our staircase, experiencing l'esprit de l'escalier, *whispering to myself: my uncertainty is the only thing that could have saved me from your death drive.*

The rat arrived expecting almonds but whatever is here is otherwise—something acrid that incinerates the tongue. Unwilling to swallow, the rat returns it to the earth.

SUBMINIATURES

Dozens of public databases, hundreds of pages, thousands of listings. Each features the often smiling face of a missing person, or the vestiges of unidentified remains. Some of the missing have been gone so long that their photos are sepia-toned to a sunset hour. Others have vanished so recently that you can match the digital images of them to active social media profiles. Others still are so obscure that there are no photographs of them, and so they have had to be sketched from memory. Even these sketched figures are not as obscure as the found but nameless dead, whose likenesses can only be photographed, drawn, or molded from autopsy. In some instances, the recovered dead get no human image whatsoever, and instead scraps of clothing stand in metonymically for the form they once adorned.

These thousands do not represent the extent of the chaos. Elsewhere, in archives invisible to the public, lay untold numbers of other missing and unidentified persons from across the country, no one even bothering to count them all, never mind compile a complete and comprehensive list of their particularities.

Limn had always supposed it would be difficult to disappear yourself or someone else, a presumption that was only hardened by so many true crime documentaries, which make it seem as though the whole world is crisscrossed by ley lines of skin cells, hair roots, bodily fluids, and singular synthetic fibres that render it possible to trace every significant passage between one person and another. Human beings as complicated snails, writing out their routes in elaborated slime.

Now, here, in the library, fitfully parsing every last ambiguous listing, Limn is convinced that disappearing must be terrifyingly easy if so many people are able to pull it off, especially since most of them probably manage it without ever intending to. Forward, back, forward, back, Limn flips between pages, sweeping across unfamiliar faces, skimming measurements that repeat into meaninglessness. Inches away, Mal fidgets in a matching, inflexible chair, head bent phoneward, performing the same laborious internet scroll, a proofreader for Limn's analysis. On the opposite side sits Slip, clicking through scans of microfiche and scrutinizing the innumerable irrelevant newspaper articles on an archaically large computer monitor. When they'd first arrived at the library, the kids introduced Slip to the missing persons databases, and Slip primed the kids on microfiche, but in the end they found that they proceeded more quickly by working in the medium to which they felt most accustomed, with an agreement to consult one another if they happened upon an item of interest, of which there are several:

1.   "It's too bad you didn't get there sooner and find more than just bones," Mal says to Slip. "If someone finds a body, with flesh, the police can provide useful details to the public. Take this person, for example, who is described as having, and I quote, *hairy legs*."

"Pity," Slip says.

"Don't a lot of people have hairy legs?" Limn asks earnestly.

2.　"This person wore *distinctive shorts*," Limn says.

"What's distinctive about them?" Mal asks.

"They've got some red and blue stripes on them I guess?"

"Like your tetras."

"Yeah. Kind of."

"It's a more useful description than the one I'm reading, which says that the person often wore black socks and blue jeans."

Limn turns to Slip. "Did you ever find any clothing with the bones?"

"No."

"Don't you think that's weird?"

Slip looks to the mineral fibre suspended ceiling tiles overhead, just an absent gaze, not really seeing them, for they are so quotidian, such a lacklustre harbour grey, that it is difficult to give them much consideration. Yet they are made of: wool spun from molten rock; glass fibres twined with plastic; perlite, born in a volcano, bubbly as pumice stone, *spuma maris,* the froth of the sea; and, coincidentally, newspaper. A cosmopolis hangs over their heads.

"Yes," Slip finally admits. "It's sort of weird."

"At first I found it unbelievable that dead bodies could have sat around decaying for a year or more in the forest in a town as small as Euphoria without being discovered by anyone but you, but some of these bodies—" Mal gestures at the phone screen "—are just, like, *right there,* metres away from a road or something, and still no one finds them for ages."

"It really is amazing how much people don't notice about the world around them," Slip agrees.

3.   An embroidered frog, dirt or blood shadowing its contours, is the only emblem offered up of an unnamed newborn laid on a bench in a graveyard. Mal studies it but does not speak of it aloud.

4.   Holding the phone in the line of sight of first Slip and then Mal, Limn shows them a photo of a figure, wearing a suit, bearing a cane, and sitting on the stone post of a guardrail intended to keep the faceless public, milling at the periphery of the image, away from a grassy slope that descends sharply to a waterfall. "A photographer took this picture of a stranger. As soon as the camera was lowered, the stranger swung over the railing and out of sight. When the photographer went to investigate, the person could not be seen either on the grass or in the whirlpool below. The photographer went to the police, reported the person as missing. Suicide was suspected. But no one ever found the body. Usually people who die in the falls float downstream and show up on the river banks. I thought it was interesting so I did a bit more digging about the story and get this: police say that going over the falls and then being stuck in the water sometimes *destroys clothing*."

"Cool," Mal says.

"Well, we were just talking about how weird it is that The Corpses have no clothing," Limn points out.

"So the murderer, what, drowned them then retrieved them from the water ages later and placed them in a forest?"

"Well, no, not that necessarily. I'm just saying there can be *natural* reasons why some dead bodies don't have clothes on."

"Maybe someone just murdered them in the forest and stripped their clothes off to minimize the evidence left behind," Slip says, unimpressed.

5.   "This unidentified body was found when contractors dug up a 45-year-old cement floor in a car dealership. Dead bodies really can be anywhere, can't they," Slip marvels.

All three of them lower their eyes to stare at the carpeted floor beneath their feet. It is burnt orange.

Though of interest, none of these cases are of any discernible significance to The Corpses in the Unwood. Setting the phone on the table, Mal collapses forward melodramatically beside it, head on wrists. "What, exactly, are we looking for?"

"You've asked that like 500 times," Limn replies, watching Mal's performance regardless.

"Tell me again," Mal says.

"We're looking for anything. Everything. Nothing." Limn's answers have become increasingly gnomic with each iteration of the question. "I mean, if you find a record of someone from Euphoria, or near Euphoria, who's missing, that could be important."

"Obviously," Mal says. "But there aren't any."

"Yet," Limn adds correctively.

"Besides that, what could possibly be of interest?" Mal presses.

"Use your youthful intuition," Slip answers gruffly.

"My youthful intuition says we're wasting our time. We don't know a single fact about our person or persons. Not their age or their height or their hair colour. We can't even really be sure they are from Euphoria. They could be from somewhere else. Visiting or hiding or—"

"Dumped," Slip supplies.

"That reminds me," Limn cuts in. "Did you ever notice any damage to the bones? Marks from bullets or a knife or anything like that?"

Slip rounds on Limn. "Tell me—do I look like a coroner to you? Do I look like someone who has a medical degree? Do you suspect that I am secretly withholding key evidence and making us skim old case files without any useful direction because I am bored? Snakelike? Harebrained?"

Limn stares back, twitchy as a housefly. "I—" But already Slip is waving the smoke of the outburst away.

"That was uncalled for. I'm sorry." Without offering an explanation, Slip's attention returns to the computer screen.

What was that? Mal mouths to Limn, whose head shakes and shoulders shrug.

"Is there anything I can help with?" The three of them startle at the voice, chirpy and harmless and nerve-wracking as if it belonged to a bird who flew by accident into the basement archives of the library. "Gosh, I didn't mean to alarm you! I just wanted to see if your research was going well."

"Fantastic!" Mal replies, smiling and nodding at length.

"If you told me a bit about what you're looking for, I might be able to help," the librarian says, out of sweetness or boredom, it is difficult to discern. "I've been working here a long time. I've seen a lot of things."

Limn hitches up a vacant and defensive smile to match Mal's.

"What kind of things?"

"I don't think we need any help," Slip counters.

"All right then." The librarian's gaze lands on each of them in turn. "You just holler if you do. I'll be around."

"Thanks!" Mal says. "Bye!"

"I like librarians," Slip says, eyes locked on the computer monitor, once the librarian has disappeared up the stairs. "Sometimes they're the only people who talk to me."

"That one seemed kind of weird, though," Mal says.

"That one's always kind of weird." Slip does not elaborate.

CITIZEN SCIENCE

The neighbour had lived in the house since before the two lovers next door were born. Blue, the one whose hair was as dark as crow feathers and reflected as much light, had always been the friendlier of the pair. On the day they moved in, Blue had crossed the lawn and hopped over the recently planted shrubs that lined the neighbour's stone walkway with guileless familiarity, just to shake hands. After that, the neighbour always paid more attention to Blue than to Culver, who had a taciturn sense of decorum and could therefore, the neighbour thought at the time, be safely ignored.

It was more than an innate suspiciousness, however, that made the neighbour watchful. It was also that Blue seemed to be watching the neighbour back. A week after the lovers moved in, Blue was out on a stepladder, brush in hand, painting the window frames, covering the harsh dark grey they had been before, and lightening them to match the white stucco of the neighbour's Mediterranean style house. The neighbour felt relief. Before, the two houses had been wholly disconnected, as if they had been dropped from different continents, by pure accident, beside one another. Now there was an affinity between them. That effort to attend to the neighbourhood, to treat it as if it were a work of art and to do one's part to establish lines of continuity through it, had been maintained, at least on Blue's part. Culver never offered any evidence of effort, though it hardly mattered since the work was in any case getting done.

Even 15 years after painting the window frames, Blue had kept up that level of conscientiousness. A year before disappearing, Blue pulled up in the coupe, which glittered like a heron on the water, and emerged with the red gladioli for the lovers' front porch. The neighbour, standing in the yard, had watched with satisfaction as the flowers were settled into their ornamental pots. Afterwards, the neighbour had even offered an approving wave and nod in Blue's direction to acknowledge the obvious fact: the flowers perfectly complemented the red tiles of the neighbour's roof.

The neighbour's years of hesitant approbation remained tenable right up until the morning that the neighbour still puzzles over, more than a year after it happened. It was early, and the sky, a pre-sun periwinkle, provided light enough to see, if dimly. The neighbour stood at the generous living room window, which arched like a curious eyebrow, sipping a cup of black tea in complete silence, as preparation for a morning of birdwatching.

Despite its name, birdwatching requires more than just eyes. In the distance between land and sky, through the median strip of clouds and leaves, some winged things are easier to hear than see. That was why the neighbour habitually contemplated dead air before birdwatching—it was a way of tightening the skin of the eardrums. Into that stillness, on that peculiar morning, the sound of the lovers' front door opening impinged. The neighbour expected, if anyone, Culver, who did not normally leave the house in the night but was often up earlier than Blue. Culver could be seen sometimes, around 7:00 a.m. or so, the time when the neighbour, if staying home that day, would be pecking at cornflakes at the kitchen table.

It was Blue who walked out, however. The neighbour set the cup of tea down noiselessly onto the sill, as if it were a distraction to hold. Of the two lovers, Blue had always been the later riser, rarely seen out of doors before 10:00 a.m. Hair cropped especially short those days, Blue looked more than ever like a crow, a species the laity tends to regard, at best, as a crop pest, and at worst, as a morbid symbol of bad luck and death. Like most birdwatchers, the neighbour was unconcerned with such pedestrian troubles and superstitions. Crows, for the neighbour, were a curiosity. They conspired to steal food from otters. They fashioned tools from bits of wood and probed holes in fences looking for spiders to swallow. They were clever; the neighbour respected them for that.

As the neighbour watched, Blue glided swiftly down the driveway, hands in pockets, a white, collared shirt flapping loosely against Blue's torso.

"You'll catch a chill," the neighbour tutted, though no one was close enough to hear it. "Where's your coat?"

At the end of the driveway, Blue turned left, walking down the middle of the road, straight past the neighbour's house.

"Where are you going, young one?" the neighbour whispered, as Blue disappeared from sight.

Weeks passed. The neighbour blamed Culver for driving Blue away, and ceased to take any tender interest in the goings-on of that domicile. Without Blue, the house became dull and unkempt, a reality that was all too plain, for though the hedge between their houses had grown well and high over the years, it was not high enough for complete indifference. The neighbour's casual attentiveness to the lovers' home was, rather abruptly, replaced by resentment.

MAGIC LANTERNS

"What if we treated the bones like lost pets?" Limn suggests.

"What does that even mean?" Mal asks.

"We could put up signs around town. *Found: one (or possibly more) human skeletons in the forest. Call to claim.*"

"Are you joking?"

"Obviously," Limn says, absently beginning to sketch a poster. "But also, maybe not."

"I don't follow." Mal's eyebrows crease.

"Clearly we're not going to literally put flyers up all over town."

"Oh good."

"People would see us," Slip says. "And who would attend the phone?"

"A murderer might call and try to get the bones back to conceal the evidence," Mal adds.

"Sure," Limn agrees. "But what if we just set up a website, anonymously, with an email where people could send us tips?"

"No," Slip says. "Absolutely not."

"Why?" Limn asks.

"One: that will possibly, maybe even probably, attract the attention of the police and unless you two are web geniuses, which I have reason to doubt, they'll find out it was us. Two: there is no possible useful information that strangers on the internet could give us. You'll just get a lot of sob stories from people looking for their missing loved ones and we'll have to say, *Well, sorry, we can't confirm whom these bones belong to.* At which point the sender will probably get angry and call—who now?"

"The police," Limn answers grudgingly.

"Right. Who will track us down. So, we're not doing it."

"I think you just underestimate the power of the internet because you're—" Limn falters before the end of the sentence—"from another generation."

"You two have been all over the internet and what have you found there?" Slip scoffs. "Case after case that can't be solved. Not very persuasive, in my opinion."

"And what have you found with your antique magic lantern, your last-century holdover technology?" Occasionally, Limn becomes rather eloquent when irate, and Mal beams approval.

"Don't be impatient," Slip scolds.

"Don't be a hypocrite," Limn retorts.

"How am I being a hypocrite?"

"Blaming *us* and *the internet* for the fact that this case isn't solved. You never should have touched the bones after you found them—"

"Would you keep your voice down."

"You should have called the police straightaway. Instead, you contaminated the crime scene."

"We don't even know if there was a crime. A hiker could have died in the woods."

"But if there *was* a crime we're unlikely to ever find out who's responsible because most of the evidence will be disputable, if not inadmissible, thanks to your inability to let other people do their jobs."

"Maybe if they'd done their jobs and found the missing person, or persons, a little sooner, it wouldn't be up to me to figure out how to manage this."

"You didn't have to manage anything. You just had to leave it alone. You could've even called in an anonymous tip to help them find the bodies. Do you think we believed your bullshit about not wanting to become a suspect? That was an excuse. Maybe you even convinced yourself it was true. But you've been selfish this whole time. Selfish and impulsive. So don't sit there and try to dispense advice to *me* about how to behave."

"Uh-huh," Slip replies. "If I had called the police there would be no mystery for you to help with and then what would you have done with yourselves this whole time?" Slip flexes tender knees, preparing to rise, if needed. The kids only sit in resigned silence. "Are you finished berating me now?"

"Sure," Limn mutters. "I've said my piece."

"I would say *the past is the past,* but that's not really true is it?" By this, Slip means something like *the past is the infrastructure of the present.* "The point is, I can't change what's already happened. So, knowing what I've done, do you want to continue working on this with me or not?" *And the present is the infrastructure of the future.* The kids exchange glances.

"Yeah, we'll keep working with you," Mal says.

"It's just a bit unbearable when you get, like, self-righteous about it," Limn adds.

Still nettled but needing the help, or, one might argue, the company, Slip compromises with an insult the kids are unlikely to understand: "Okay popinjays."

KEW

Amid September's waning temperatures, the kids announce that they have exhausted the relevant missing persons databases. Slip regards this waypost with both relief and alarm. Back in school as they now are, the kids' capacity for assistance is limited; it is better to have them be through the thick of the work. But Slip is alone again, trawling through reels of microfiche that, while decisively finite, vastly exceed foreseeable energy and time, and so seem otherwise.

"Is there anything we can do?" Limn asks Slip as they pass each other one Saturday on the main road of the trailer park. Limn is coming into the park—from where, at this early hour?—while Slip is leaving the park for another day at the library.

"I'm not really sure." The three of them cannot use the microfiche reader at the same time. As for the internet, Slip has heard of entire online realms, but responds to them probably the same way other people feel when they read about fantastical lands in books, with their names that are familiar in syllable only, characters recognizable by their archetypes but not by the details of their identities. "I'll let you know if I think of anything."

"I've been hovering around some forums," Limn says. "Local and regional ones, crime ones. There are lots of reports of people who've gone missing but never really made it onto police radar, so they don't show up on the official databases. Like maybe they're transient, or for some reason the police believe they left voluntarily, and they won't even look into it, never mind treat it as an official case. There are no cases from around here that I've read about yet though."

"That's great," Slip says. "That's something." The two of them study their shoes.

"Okay, see you around." Limn heads off in the direction of home.

"Sure," Slip replies, belatedly.

Kew. Like a cue. A warning word, sharp and musical. It comes from a dark-eyed junco, feathered charcoal over snow, sheltering in a shrub by the side of the road. The dark-eyed junco is a bird who once had seven names but is now confined to one.

"Cue? A cue for what? For treason?" Slip laughs.

Kew, kew, kew.

"Just tell me what to do. I can't take a hint."

CATCH AND RELEASE

"Another day of fiche-ing?" a voice inquires over Slip's shoulder. "That's my word for it. Like fishing, but with microfiche. Ha ha." It is the librarian, the one who is always around, shelving books or retrieving items from the archives, but never working the front desk. Slip suspects this is a purposeful choice, though whether on the part of management or the librarian it is hard to say and, either way, it elevates Slip's sense of affinity between them. Though the librarian is younger, Slip suspects a world wariness, which is not to say world weariness, there—the apprehensiveness of an adult who spent childhood being tacitly excluded, but never explicitly rejected.

"I'll probably be here 'til I've read every last newspaper you have," Slip says.

"Are you trying to set a world record or something?" The librarian giggles. "Most out-of-date newspapers read in a single year?"

"Just looking for something I don't expect to find."

"I wish you'd tell me what it is. You know, I've read most of these papers myself over the course of my 23 years here."

"Have you?"

"Indeed, I have. Research for my website."

"What's your website about?"

"Holding Euphoria's municipal government accountable for their social policy and fiscal choices." The librarian's head and voice drop conspiratorially. "You can't trust institutions, right? And the problem with city government is not so much that it's secretive, though of course, it often is, but the real problem is that almost no one cares enough to compile and study all of the information about it, and the ones who do are usually getting paid to make the bureaucracy run smoothly, so usually they're not going to hold anyone accountable or try to propose reform."

"But you care."

"*Deeply.* I'm the gadfly of Euphoria." There is a self-satisfied smile on the librarian's face. Though referring to oneself as a biting insect would ordinarily smack of self-deprecation, Slip is impressed by the unexpected but obvious pride with which the librarian delivers this comparison.

"Maybe," Slip admits, "you can help me after all. I'm trying to find…examples…of people who have gone missing but who haven't been officially declared missing by the police." The librarian nearly trembles with glee.

"Local people? People from afar? Both?"

"I suppose starting with people from around Euphoria will suffice for now," Slip says noncommittally, as though this were some more general project that Slip was, upon consideration, willing to narrow temporarily. "Then we could branch out as needed."

"Branch out! Ha ha. Is that a library joke?"

"No."

"Disappointing. But regardless, I *can* help you. Surely I can." The librarian reaches into a pocket, pulls out a business card, and hands it to Slip. "That's my website at the bottom. I think you'll find lots of information that will be of interest to you, so take a look around. For now, though, I do specifically remember one rather recent case. Let's see if we can find it." The librarian motions for Slip to get out of the chair and commandeers the computer. "I think it would have been last year in the summer…Ah! Yes, here's my post about it." Slip follows the librarian's finger to the screen, scans the text. It describes a long-time resident whose two friends disappeared. Police refused to help. *What's the point of police at all? So much town money funnelled to them but why?* It is unclear whether this latter opinion is that of the resident being profiled, or of the original article's author, or of the librarian, or if it is shared by all of them.

"Do you have a phone number, or some kind of contact information, for this person?" Slip asks.

"No. It was just something I read in the paper and did a little write-up on for my blog. Here's the date I posted it." The librarian points to the line above the title. "The article probably would have come out in the paper about a week or so before?"

The librarian's estimate proves correct, as Slip is able to determine after an hour or so of skimming that week's editions. The article in question was published on the Saturday before the blog post; it was front page news, in fact. Slip remembers scanning the microfiche of that issue, but had dismissed the cover story as irrelevant—it focused on local assessments of police efficacy in light of the proposed municipal budget, which included a large increase to police funding—and so had skipped its continuation entirely. The relevant quote from the resident only appeared after a jump. It was a scant line, practically a footnote, in a barely noticeable couple of paragraphs on an interior page. There is hardly any detail in the article beyond what the blog post offered, save for the unfamiliar name of the resident. Slip prints off a copy of the article to bring to the kids, before tracking down the librarian again.

"I found it," Slip says. "Thank you for your help. And you're sure you know nothing more about this person?" Slip presses, holding out the original article to refresh the librarian's memory.

"Only as much as you," the librarian replies. "Sorry." Slip nods, checks the clock on the wall, noting that school will be out in an hour.

"Thank you again for your help," Slip says. "I have to go now."

"Did you find what you needed?"

"Maybe."

"Will you be back tomorrow?"

"Who can say."

MAYHEM

Waking to a desolate bed for the first time in 16 years, Culver thought that Blue must have ruined their carefully laid plans by going downstairs for a glass of water in the middle of the night and dying alone by mistake. A freak heart attack, perhaps, or an aneurysm triggered by a muffled fall. Blood pulsed in Culver's vigilant ears.

Outside, a neighbour's dog barked, a coarse and woolly sound. Inside, tiny drops of water escaped the faucet and landed tinnily in the kitchen sink, as happened often when the tap had been flicked off carelessly. Blue hated the repetitive plinking of a leaking faucet—could hear it, and hate it, in fact, even from other floors, or the far side of the house. If the tap was left dripping, Blue must not be home.

After 128 heartbeats, Culver sat up and called out, *Where are you?* just in case Blue had tripped and could not get up to turn off the tap, then counted another 32 beats before rising and methodically inspecting the house, room by room. In the ensuite, the towels and toothbrushes were dry; in Blue's study, mail opened and unopened lay like fallen leaves on the desk; in the kitchen, last night's unwashed dishes loitered on the counter; in Blue's jacket pocket there was still a driver's license, a debit card, a set of car and house keys; and, in their shared safe, every last dollar from the stack of emergency cash could be accounted for. When Culver turned the knob, the front door of the house sprang smoothly open, revealing the tree-lined street, which was motionless but for leaves shivering in the slight wind, and a local cat, sleek as a fish-fed seal, who promenaded along the sidewalk past their house.

The house was pristine, except the basement, where Culver found a scarcely intelligible mayhem of clues. Splashes of blood and vomit, snarls of hair, a partly depleted bottle of sodium cyanide, with its characteristic bitter almond smell. None of it necessarily belonged to Blue, but the onyx strands, splintered at the ends, the stomach contents, with rinds of salted lemon like those they had eaten the night before, were familiar.

Culver panicked, then quieted, calmed by insight.

"It doesn't make sense," Culver said assuredly, surveying the scene once more. Cyanide poisoning would explain the vomit, but after ingestion death would descend within minutes, not enough time for Blue to run very far. And why would the ground be covered in blood and hair, as though Blue had grappled with an attacker? There had been no disturbances in the house the night before. Furthermore, Culver was sure that Blue was not suicidal, not really. With Culver's gentle prodding, Blue might walk passively into the Unwood and unto death. But active and independent self-destruction? It was unfathomable. Culver could contrive only two explanations for the chaos in their basement. Either Blue was incapable of staging a convincing death scene—unlikely—or else Blue wanted to create an impossible tangle of confusion and suspicion, so that Culver would never go to the police for help finding Blue, too afraid of becoming an obvious suspect in a possible murder.

Culver felt secure in assuming, then, that the scene had been faked, and began to generate a list of events that could have followed the staging:

- Blue left the house to die alone.
- Blue left the house to die with someone else.
- Blue left the house and was still alive, with or without someone else.

In all instances, Culver had been betrayed. In all cases, Blue was probably not coming back. The brief, serene relief of epiphany was swept away by an incoming storm of fury. How could Blue leave? At that very time? They were supposed to be grieving their lost child together. They were supposed to be dying together, interlocked like the roots of two trees who had grown for years beside one another. Instead, Blue had brought down the axe, severed the crux. Worse yet, Blue had slunk away without a word, which, in Culver's opinion, was the most faithless and cowardly act, for it showed that Blue did not believe Culver could ever understand what was happening. Or, worse still, that Blue simply did not care whether Culver understood.

The storm subsided, leaving behind an empty sky. Unwilling to remove the mess in the basement, Culver walked slowly upstairs to the living room and cowered, face pressed into the corner of the couch. Spectres of Blue came upon Culver like a migraine, possessing Culver's entire body. In the aura, there were faces, barely recognizable. Some were the faces of the two lovers when they were young. There were, too, tremolo notes of catgut from Blue's violin.

Time passed, but Culver went on being exhausted, weak, numb. Pained by the sunlight dripping into the room. Throbbing veins echoed, fist on flesh. Explicit memory bled into muscle memory. Culver reached for Blue and grasped only words. *Hiraeth. Saudade. Sehnsucht.* The words stretched out toward experience and fell like fledglings in the air.

Culver wanted an impossibility, which was very much like wanting nothing, and in that vacuum, even the image of death lost its glamour, becoming as tawdry as life.

RESIDUAL

Staggering out of the haze of sleep, Culver should be forgiven for reacting exaggeratedly to being alone in an empty bed, since it was only the second time in 16 years that Culver had woken alone, not knowing where Blue was. Normally, Culver would have been told in advance that Blue was going to be away. Otherwise, Culver would be able to hear Blue shuffling about downstairs, on the rare morning that Blue rose first. Instead, Culver, not yet remembering the events of the previous day, startled and bolted upright, catastrophizing, wondering if Blue might be in the midst of an emergency, might even be dying.

Recollection returned within seconds, but those seconds felt endless. It was only after leaping from the sheets and lurching toward the door of the room they used to share, that Culver remembered what had come to pass and collapsed shoulder-first against the frame. Yesterday was the first day without Blue, and it had been marked by the fury of sudden realization, then the numb shock that follows a bombshell. Tomorrow, perhaps, or the day after, or next week, the reification would come, and the awful event would lose the last pearling glimmer of dream, and would turn sundry, fixed, habitual.

In the interim, however, Culver was living in the immediate aftermath, amid the murk and tumult of the dust and ashes slowly blowing away, faced with the terrible promise of soon seeing remnants and damage clearly.

Down to the basement Culver went, collecting supplies from cabinets and water from the sink along the way. Beneath the amber glow of low-watt incandescent bulbs, Culver knelt, pressed a white sheet to the floor, scoured the cream carpet with a scrub brush and a shimmering slime of dish soap, then soaked it with hydrogen peroxide until it was a foaming mouth. Splatters of lemon-yellow milkshake made of rind and vinegar, dried-up ponds of pomegranate turned to maple syrup, these were rendered invisible, if not undetectable, by the cleaning. The once-white sheet now held the transferred, washed-out pastels of vomit and blood.

Culver collected by hand the thousands of head hairs threaded through the warp and weft of the carpet wool and lifted several of them up to the light. Nearly every black strand, obviously deliberately extracted, was a complete entity that had retained its root, its source of telltale DNA. Investigators would easily be able to discern to whom the hair had belonged.

"The real cruelty is how thoroughly you planned this" Culver said to an absent Blue. "You did not leave in a fit of pique. You schemed against me." Into a black satin bag Culver placed the folded sheet, smelling of the detritus of human life, and the tumbleweed of fallen tresses.

Actual tumbleweeds form when a plant—sometimes amaranth, the flower of immortality—severs from its roots and, though technically dead, continues to move, scattering its seeds. Some tumbleweeds have done more; they have blocked roads, they have buried houses. Figurative and now safely shrouded, that tumbleweed snarl of Blue's hair seemed unlikely to migrate, less likely still to wreak devastation. To the cotton and hair in the bag, Culver added the small bottle of sodium cyanide, half-empty. Death by poison was an eventuality they had never discussed, and of which Culver would have, of course, never approved, for it fell under the category of violence. And hurt, damage, injury, Culver thought resentfully, were the very indignities they had both wanted to avoid, the very reasons why they were seeking respite in the Unwood. Blue, probably intentionally, Culver thought, was taking revenge. For what, exactly? Because Culver had presumed to be the architect this time, to draw the blueprints, to design their exit door? Blue's reprisal was the staging of a crime scene, perversely pretending that their relationship had ended in brutality.

Upstairs, Culver retrieved two plastic bags from the kitchen and took them, along with the satin bag, into Blue's study to collect the handwritten letter, which Culver had first read yesterday morning, though Blue had composed it some indeterminate amount of time before that. Culver set down the bags.

"There are a lot of lies here, Blue," Culver said, flipping through the pages of the letter. "You make it sound like I was pressuring you into dying with me. You play the martyr when all along you held the cards. Surely you knew I would have done anything you asked of me, if only you were capable of asking decisively."

Culver wadded the papers together, smaller than a lamb's heart, and placed them inside the first plastic bag. "This letter contains nothing I recognize as you, and I won't let it rest beside your hair, your blood. These pages deserve to be trashed."

If Culver thought about it, though, there had been several hints that Blue's first instinct in a crisis would most likely be flight.

There were, for instance, the first six months after they started sleeping together, when Blue would wait until Culver was unconscious, and, only then, creep wordlessly from Culver's apartment and into the anonymous darkness. Culver endured that treatment silently for a good long while before making a fuss.

"Leaving already?" Culver had said one night, startling Blue, who was lacing up shoes in the pitch black doorway.

"What are you doing up?" Blue asked.

"We talk for hours every day but you can't even say goodnight before you leave? As if this were," Culver grimaced, "a hookup."

"Did I wake you? I tried to be quiet."

"It feels like you don't really want to be with me."

"Oh Culver, you know that's not true."

"Then what is the truth?"

Blue opened the door and slid through it without answering.

When Blue called as usual the next day, Culver kept waiting for Blue to make up some plausible excuse, at least, but none was offered. It took Blue a week to return to the subject.

"I love you: that's the problem," Blue declared out of nowhere as sound blared around them. They had gone to a rowdy and crowded music venue—a converted church in a nearby city—to see a glitch artist Culver liked, but it was Blue's suggestion to go. Culver thought a breakup was imminent, that Blue was artistically using glitch music's so-called *aesthetic of failure* as a kind of pathetic fallacy backdrop for their own interpersonal collapse. But Culver had not been expecting *love* to be the problem. "This is the first time I've ever been in love with anyone," Blue continued, "and I feel, if I'm not careful, that our skin will just melt, and we'll fuse together."

So that was why Blue pried them apart nightly. "Are you breaking up with me?" Culver asked.

"No, of course not," Blue said. "If I wanted to break up with you, I would just leave and never come back."

Culver did not say anything, and after that Blue began to stay through the night sometimes.

Yes, Blue was prone to flight. Years after the incident at the concert, Blue and Culver had found a rabbit in their garden. It was hurt, obviously in pain, wide-eyed and breathing fast. They could see its organs protruding from a deep gash in its belly.

"We have to kill it," Culver said. "Put the poor thing out of its misery."

"No," Blue said.

"You can't repair this kind of damage," Culver insisted.

Blue stood up abruptly and rushed into the house, leaving Culver alone to stroke the rabbit's chestnut fur, and swiftly snap its unresisting neck.

Culver returned from reverie and went to look out the window, twisting the loose handles of the bag around and around on themselves, before tugging them roughly into a tightly-wound knot, as if to trap the perceived falsehoods of the record inside. A sterling sky articulated the possibility of rain but did not swear to it.

Turning back to Blue's desk, Culver removed stacks of correspondence and sent them careening into the second plastic bag with a terse sweep of the arm. Blue's laptop was also on the desk. Culver booted it up, checked the email. Automatic replies had been enabled, which Culver took as a further affront, additional evidence of Blue's maliciously deliberate departure.

Please note that, effective immediately, I will not be able to respond to any professional inquiries, due to an unforeseen family situation. Your patience and understanding are greatly appreciated.

"Unforeseen," Culver spat. "Family," Culver said with a bitter bark of laughter. "Such subtle irony, Blue. No one but me would see it. And this, I suppose, leaves you free to disappear. The display in the basement was for me, to warn me to stay away. This email should dissuade any of your professional contacts from being too nosy. We both know your parents won't expend much energy contacting you. Who else is there?"

Anger, Culver thought, is just an ugly scab on a deeper wound. Alone in the house, Culver felt as pitiful as a house pet left behind in a move, staring forlornly around the vacant rooms, hissing at shadows. But Culver was not a house pet and resolved to behave like a creature with thumbs and a car.

Back downstairs, Culver opened a map and traced two routes with a fingertip: the first to the landfill, to dispose of the two plastic bags, and the second to a nameless stretch of beach just north of Lac Lemot's largest and most popular beach, to bury the black satin bag. Culver packed the plastic bags and a shovel from the garage into the trunk of the car, and let the black satin bag ride up front.

"Our last little trip together, Blue," Culver said to the bag, slumping in the passenger seat.

ACCIDENT

It looks like an accident. A small adult, fully dressed in black work boots, blue jeans, and red flannel, is lying on the deck at the edge of the trailer park's pool that, while not yet officially closed for the season, has been kept vacant by the nip of near-autumn.

"Is that…?" Limn asks.

"I think so," Mal replies. They break into a trot, hurrying along the main road of the trailer park toward the pool.

"Hey!" Limn calls when they are a few metres away. Slip rises.

"Oh good, you're home from school. I have news."

"Why are you lurking by the water like some kind of kelpie?" Mal asks.

"We thought something was wrong," Limn adds in a huff.

"On the contrary," Slip retrieves a scrap of paper from within a shirt pocket and hands it to Limn. "I think we've finally made progress." On the paper there is a name.

"Who is this?" Mal asks.

"That's what we need to find out," Slip replies. "I would do it myself, but it's not in the phone book, so…" Whether that is supposed to be a joke is unclear to Limn.

"So you want us to look this name up online?" Limn asks.

"Do you think we'll find it?" Slip asks.

"Probably," Mal says. "Maybe."

"No one's home right now at my place," Limn offers and Slip waves it off.

"We'll go to the library. I'm not hanging around your trailers without your parents home."

"You're back already!" the librarian says brightly when Slip skitters into the library with the kids.

"Very helpful, you were very helpful," Slip answers in passing.

The three of them huddle around a free computer, Limn poised over the keyboard.

"Look it up, look it up," Slip mutters.

"I am looking it up," Limn hisses back. "Must be a very common name. Lot of matches." Diligently, Limn calls up site after site, hoping for some further hint at an identity.

"Add 'Euphoria' to your search terms," Mal suggests, impatient after whole minutes of skimming. "Try an image search instead," Mal adds.

Pages of photos rush past them like landscape through a car window.

"Wait!" Mal says, pointing to a minuscule, grainy photo. "That person looks familiar somehow." Zooming in, then out again, Limn struggles to make sense of the pixels.

"It's so blurry it looks like one of those photo mosaics." Limn leans back, leans forward, squints.

"Well it's no one I know," Slip says.

"Oh my fuck." Mal taps several times on Limn's forearm. "You know who that is."

"I don't."

"Yes, you do."

"Who is it?" Slip asks.

"Let's go see," Mal says.

Limn falters. "I see it! I see it!"

The kids stand. Slip tries again. "Where are we going?"

"To Utopia," Limn answers.

"It doesn't exist," says the librarian, who happens to be walking by.

SWARMING UTOPIA

Stamped onto the burlap sack are the lithe, green-limbed lines of a tree, flaring into a thick wool of white flowers, and the word *Thrace*—the name of the company perhaps, though it's not familiar to Fir—curls cursively through the tree's topmost leaves. Drawing an almond from the bag, Fir splits its molluscan shell with a nutcracker, and promptly drops both seed and tool when the bell over the door of Utopia Video tolls to tell of incoming customers.

Flitting toward the counter are the very teenagers Fir has been waiting to see, shadowed by an unfamiliar person at least four times their age. They are a triad that fills Fir with both delight and fear.

"I was right!" Mal buzzes. "Oh, I was right!"

Onto the counter in front of Fir, Limn places two pieces of paper, both computer printouts. To the left is a partial newspaper page featuring the continuation of an article about the local police force budget that Fir has to read to recognize, and to the right is a grainy photo that displays one of Fir's past selves.

"This is you." Limn points to the photo. "This is also you." Limn points to the article. "Right?"

"You must have had to do a deep dive for these," Fir says. "Were you looking for information about me?"

Slip, who has been standing behind the teenagers, taps their shoulders so they move aside, and steps forward. Palms flat on the counter, Slip studies Fir. "You've lost someone. We've found someone."

"What does that mean? Who did you find? Where?"

"I can show you."

"Hold on a minute," Mal interrupts. "You're going to take this random to see the bones that you still won't let us see even though we've been helping you for months? That is so, so…uncool."

"Has anyone you loved disappeared on you?" Slip turns first to Mal, then to Limn.

"You'll notice that this one—" Mal gestures toward Limn "—is being raised by a single parent. So yes."

"That's different," Limn says. "The deadbeat just left us. No one shrugged off this mortal coil."

"Shuffled," Fir corrects.

"And when did you last hear from the deadbeat, exactly?" Mal asks. "Months ago, right?"

"Several months ago now, I guess."

"How can you be sure where the deadbeat is now then? That the deadbeat is even still alive?"

Dazed as a pigeon denied by a window, Limn stares at Mal. "I never thought about it like that. I just assumed…it's not like it's out of the ordinary…we rarely get more than two calls a year."

"But you can't be sure, can you?"

"You don't really think…"

"No, I'm just saying we know what it's like to lose people." Mal flicks sharp eyes back to Slip, who gives no indication of being moved by this development.

"If you were all listening closely," Slip says, "you'd have noticed that I said I can show Fir what I've found. I didn't say I've decided yet whether I will."

"Show what, though?" Fir asks.

"The bones in the woods," Slip replies.

"Are you sure they're human?" Fir asks apprehensively.

"Hard to argue with a skull," Slip replies.

"A skull? Only one skull?" Fir's brow furrows.

"Yes, just one," Slip says. "Why, were you expecting more?"

Fir sinks down to sit on the floor behind the counter, fixating on the geometric cool of the tiles. What had Fain said the last time Fir collapsed like this? *You've got to stop doing that, or you'll become a neutron star.* Fir is faintly aware, but does not care, that the three strangers are leaning forward over the counter to stare with concern.

"This is going well," Mal says.

"Pass this over," Slip mumbles to Limn, whose long arm in its green sleeve stretches toward Fir like a stem of asparagus. Fir takes it. A trailer park address has been handwritten on the scrap of paper.

"Pay me a visit when your shift is over," Slip says.

"Okay," Fir agrees, dazed.

"We'll talk things through. Decide what to do next."

"All right."

"In the meantime, maybe we should leave you to your work," Slip says. "You might get a customer."

As the three of them walk out of the store, the chimes ring, and Mal says something like, *What exactly is our role going to be? We're not just sitting backstage after this, you know.*

THE ALMOND TREE

The story of the almond tree, like most stories, is a shapeshifter that can, and sometimes must, take several forms, particularly as it grows older. Within each iteration, there live two people, and they are lovers, and that is all you really need to know about them. You certainly don't need their names, for though the story is theirs, and its events happened to them—in fact, keep happening to them—the events could have happened to anyone, and they still might.

The first time the story happened, one of the lovers was set to depart on a journey, while the other was to remain homebound. The homebound lover gave the journeying lover a gift, a small ornamental casket, a memento mori, and said, *Open this only if you are not coming home to me.* In the middle of the voyage, the journeying lover was caught in a terrible storm and washed up on an unintended shore. There the journeying lover opened the casket and was possessed by its image of demise. In horror, the journeying lover took flight from the island and sped, inadvertently, directly toward death. For ages, the remaining lover waited, withering with despair, limbs turning brittle as those of a dry tree, until both of the lovers had perished.

Most people did not like this version, so the story had to retell itself anew.

The second time the story happened, the journeying lover left and was delayed, unable to reach the homebound lover for a long time, and if the journeying lover was delayed because of a fixation on death, this was a coincidence and not the kind of preoccupation that made love impossible. Nevertheless, the homebound lover had to linger, waiting for the journeying lover to come home, and in this waiting withered to a tree. A friend saw what had happened, and took pity, and called the sun and the rain to attend. Under the friend's dutiful care, the lover who had turned into a tree was able to persist but would not blossom. Finally, one day, the journeying lover returned, and wept with regret over the roots until the lover-turned-tree bloomed with white flowers. That summer, almonds fell like confetti in the field.

The second version was more popular, and some people still tell it today, though the story has since gone on, re-envisioning itself, never quite resolved.

AMBIT

"Do you think this is it?" Fain asks from the driver's seat. "Do you think you're about to find what you've been looking for?"

"I'm not sure if it is and I'm not sure if I want it to be," Fir replies, eyes fixed on the side of the road as if it were the shoulder of someone familiar.

"I've lived in this town for, what, over ten years now? And I can't remember ever being inside this trailer park. I might never have even gone down this street," Fain said.

"Why would you, I guess. It's not like the road goes anywhere. Just a dead end."

"A dead end? I hope not."

"Ha."

"You've been here before, of course," Fain observes as they turn into the park.

"That was about the only time."

"What does it feel like to be a kid growing up here?"

"Or to be an old person dying here?"

"Literally marginalized. On the periphery of Euphoria."

More lonely, less lonely. Higher risk, lower risk. Louder, quieter. Fir tests and dismisses possible answers. "Probably it's not that much different from living with six roommates."

"Maybe not." Fain pauses. "Did you tell them you were bringing a friend?"

"No. But I didn't swear to come alone either."

"Where do you think I should park?"

Fir shrugs. Fain manoeuvres the car so it sits mostly on the corner of Slip's lot, tires just barely trespassing on the adjacent roadway. Slip is standing at the trailer door, staring at Fain's car.

"Who's that?" Slip asks Fir while pointing at Fain, as soon as they have opened the doors of the car to get out.

"This is my friend." Aware of how generic that sounds, Fir embellishes to compensate. "My collaborator. My accomplice. My spine. My true blue." Fir blushes at that last word, which is significant beyond what Fir intended. Even if Fir has spent years pining passionately after Blue, in some ways Fir and Fain are closer than Fir and Blue ever were.

"Hi," Fain says to Slip with a tentative wave.

"This isn't a hiking troupe," Slip complains, as the kids materialize behind Fir and Fain.

"What's going on?" Mal asks.

"Who's that?" Limn scrutinizes Fain.

"Doesn't matter," Slip says. "I'm only taking one of you with me. Let's go." Slip starts walking, tapping Fir on the shoulder in passing.

"You can…you don't have to…" Fir starts to say to Fain.

"I'll be here when you need a ride home. Or if anything happens," Fain whispers back.

"You don't have to…"

"I know."

"Thanks."

"Good luck." Fain's hand touches Fir's arm, then flutters away like a butterfly.

TAKE THY FORM FROM OFF MY DOOR

"We still don't know who you are," Mal says to Fain with that slightly haughty affectation reserved for adults whose trustworthiness has yet to be proven.

"It's not important," Fain replies, glancing briefly at the two teenagers before walking off in the direction of Fir and Slip, who are by now 20 metres ahead.

"Where are we going?" Mal asks as the kids move to follow. No answer from Fain, not even an acknowledgement that a question has been asked.

"Where are *you* going?" Limn tries. Still nothing.

Last of the five, Limn observes the wobbly formation of the flock ahead. Slip, Fir, Fain, Mal, Limn, each tailing the person directly ahead. Cranes stretching their necks toward an invisible forthcoming.

When they reach the end of the road that runs past The Singing Frog, Slip and Fir ignore the checkerboard warning sign and vanish into the thick of the woods. Fain stops, snaps a photo, and turns back toward the trailer park, walking through the sightline of the kids who have paused to watch and consider.

"Who should we go with?" Mal whispers to Limn.

"This wouldn't even be happening without us, and yet we're being left out of it," Limn mumbles.

"It's insulting," Mal agrees.

"Yeah." Limn is desperate to be let in on the truth. Still, that morning in Utopia Video, Fir became the first adult to ever melt like a burned-out candle to the floor in front of Limn, and that seems equally important to consider. Then, of course, there is the morbid lore of the Unwood. With a sigh, Limn shadows Fain back to the trailer park.

"Okay then." Mal sighs, close behind Limn.

The kids find Fain sitting in the car outside Slip's trailer, leaning back against the headrest, eyes closed. Sometimes, after a long shift, Limn's parent dozes on the couch and strikes the same cadaverous pose, an expression of exhaustion so complete that it approaches death. Eyelids too tired to flicker, lungs scantly respiring.

"Hey!" Mal raps on the window, nettlesome as a raven. It is too late for Limn to say shut up, or to pry them both away from the scene. Fain opens one leery eye to regard the teenagers, Mal leaning an elbow on the car, Limn fidgeting a few paces away.

"Hello," Fain says.

"Can we talk?" Mal asks.

"Go ahead." Fain does not roll down the car window but does open a second eye.

"Okay. Who are you?"

"Just a friend who's been helping Fir search for two missing people over the past year or so. Who are you?"

"We're helping Slip," Mal explains. "We're the ones who tracked down your friend, Fir. We set this whole meeting up, really."

"Good job," Fain says, straight-faced.

"So, are you just going to sit in your car until they come back?"

"I might."

"Are you mad that you couldn't go, too?"

"Why would I be mad? It's not my friends who were lost."

"People cut you out as soon as they no longer need you, don't they?"

"That's a childish assessment."

"Doesn't make it wrong."

"All right, thanks for the chat." Fain closes both eyes again, and Mal turns to Limn.

"Some people have no curiosity."

SPONTANEOUS HUMAN CESSATION

Moving through the clinging, gossamer dark of the woods, the stranger ahead of Fir is small, limbs delicate as spider legs, and invokes that familiar arachnid fear: a visceral near-terror that cannot quite be quelled even though the creature who causes it could be extinguished by a careless toe. If there is a path, they are heedless of it, forging ahead in accordance with Slip's inscrutable sense of direction. Tree branches grasp at their sleeves. Soon, Fir loses not only the intuition of space but also of time. Sunlight, such as it reaches them, is partial, diffuse—a ubiquitous, diminished radiance. Grasping for a clock, Fir finds only empty pockets, realizing with a jolt of alarm that the phone must still be in the console of Fain's car.

"Are we close yet?" Fir asks.

"If I can walk the distance, so can you," Slip replies.

Fir, who felt completely calm about the Unwood before ever stepping foot inside it, understands now how the cramped gloom of it can rile interlopers into panic.

All at once the forest changes, opens abruptly as a door, which Slip steps calmly through while Fir frets on the threshold.

"This is the Unwood," Fir says.

"Yes," Slip confirms.

"I've lived in Euphoria all my life, but I've never set foot in here before."

"You'll survive," Slip says. "Just don't stay still for too long."

Fir sucks in a huge gulp of breath and, holding it, follows Slip into the glade. Ground cover tangles around their ankles, friendly as snakes, and dry leaves hiss and crackle under their feet, but their faces and arms are free again.

"We're here," Slip declares.

"Where are the bodies?" Fir asks, and Slip points to a fallen tree directly in front of them. Fir scans the tree, perplexed. "I don't see anything."

Sighing, Slip kneels and places a hand into a hollow of the tree. Many of the bone fragments are so small that, by sight alone, Fir might have mistaken them for grey twigs or irregular pebbles, though when Fir touches them it is obvious somehow that they are bodily relics.

"Where are the personal effects, the clothes?" Fir asks.

"I never found any."

Fir scoffs at this improbable reply. But if Slip has been a graverobber there is nothing to be done about it now. "Where is the skull?"

From the centre of a nearby shrub, Slip extracts the skull and hands it to Fir, who grasps it with hands against the temples, staring into the eye sockets. At first Fir does cry—hardly the only time that has happened since Blue disappeared—but then this soundless rain is interrupted, unexpectedly, by laughter.

Slip shapes an indistinct syllable, as if about to ask a question, something like, *Why are you laughing?* before falling silent again. Someone who has lived as long as Slip can usually fathom why a grieving person might perform nonsense.

"It's such a small skull," Fir says finally.

"I suppose."

"You heard that I was looking for two people?"

"Yes."

"And I was, but I only cared about one of them."

"I see."

"The one I did not care about had the smaller head. Small, like this skull."

"Oh."

Slip steps aside, sits on a grounded tree trunk while Fir sifts forest soil through urgent fingers.

"People don't just walk naked into the woods and spontaneously die," Fir says, after exhausting the area in the immediate vicinity of the bones.

"Why not?" Slip asks.

Fir ignores the question. "You can go. I want to keep searching the area. I'll find my way out."

"Don't count on that," Slip scolds. "I'll wait."

Fir finds the last scrap of truth beneath the green arrowheaded leaves, the flowers like purple stars, the fruit red and glossy as candied cherries, of bittersweet nightshade.

"I was right," Fir says, holding the find aloft.

Slip sidles over and studies the golden ring in Fir's hand.

"1999," Slip reads. "What is it?"

"This could be Culver's class ring."

"Culver's the one you didn't like?"

"Yes."

"Couldn't it belong to any of the hundreds of people from Culver's graduating class?"

"Why would their rings be out here? They're not missing," Fir points out. "And I know it doesn't belong to Blue. This is Culver's. It has to be."

"So, you think the other one might still be alive?"

"Blue, yes."

"That's the one you liked, right?"

LAVISH

Mal and Limn have been sitting by the window of Limn's trailer for most of the afternoon, watchful as dogs left behind, and when they see Slip and Fir trudging laboriously up the park road, they go bounding out to meet them, though between the grim resolution on Fir's face and Slip's exhausted limp, they calculate that it is probably better to say nothing just yet and so fall into step at the tail of the procession.

Back at Slip's trailer, Fain is fully asleep in the car, startling awake when Fir opens the passenger door. Their eyes meet, but only the engine mutters as it comes to life. Fain waves, mostly to Slip, and they are off. The kids stand in the tire tracks left on the grass.

"Well?" Limn asks.

"Come inside, I guess," Slip replies.

Without inquiry, Slip places glasses of pineapple juice and a plate of crackers on a TV tray in front of the couch where the kids sit, a gesture which Mal appreciates immediately and Limn does not even notice.

"Well," Slip says and the kids wait, expectant. Finally, Slip continues, "No one's going to the police. It seems like that skull belongs to one of the two friends that were missing."

"Seems?" Limn repeats.

"Fir thinks it does, and that's enough for me."

"You're joking," Mal says through a mouthful of wheat dust.

"If you went to the police they could test DNA, check dental records," Limn points out. "You don't all have to resign yourselves to uncertainty just because you're—"

"What?" Slip asks.

"Old and jaded," Mal replies.

"Let's pretend someone goes to the police about this," Slip says. "Let's assume they identify the body. If it is the person we think it is, then either Fir's other friend is there in the Unwood dead as well, or else the other friend is not there and then becomes a suspect, and we still might never find out how death occurred. In either case, Fir wants it left alone."

"What if those bones don't belong to either of Fir's friends?" Limn asks. "Other people could be out there, frantic to find the person *they* care about."

Slip shrugs. "Maybe Fir needs a reason to stop searching."

"And why are you satisfied with this?" Limn presses.

"While we were in the woods, Fir told me what happened with the missing friends, and I don't feel there's anything more I need to hear. I've lived long enough to see that greater certainty than this is rarely offered."

"And what about us?" Mal asks.

"You're young. You'll find something else to do with your time."

"No, I mean, don't you think we deserve to hear the friends' story, too?"

"Sure you do. And when you're older, when there's nothing

left for you in Euphoria and you're ready to leave, I'll tell you everything. In the meantime, let's not allow the dead one's memory to become the subject of town gossip."

"What if you die before I get out of Euphoria?" Limn's voice falters.

"I'll write it down for you. I'll make sure you get it."

TOUCH ME NOT

With a crystallizing patience, refined as blankest sugar, Fain keeps a steady hand on the wheel and waits until Fir is ready to speak.

"I have to leave town," Fir says as they are driving past fields occupied only by autumn-blooming wildflowers.

"Oh?" Fain asks. "Did you get a lead?"

"Yes," Fir replies. "And no."

Lungs full, Fain brakes, pulls the car off to the side of the road, rolls down the window, and stares at the yellow blossoms that are like sleeping goldfinches in the lea.

"I believe the bones belong to Culver," Fir explains. "There was only one skull. There was a class ring there like one that belonged to Culver. I can't say for sure, but I'm satisfied that we've found as much of an answer as I need."

"Have you thought about going to the police, if the skull is obviously human?"

"I have thought about it, yes. I think our lives are complicated enough already, don't you?"

Slip, Limn, Mal, Fir, Fain, all of them could be caught up, spectators to a gruesome unveiling, dolphins in a tuna net. A sordid legacy could stick like a barnacle to the muddied skeleton of Culver. *What is Blue breathing now?* Fir wonders. *Air, fire, water, earth?* Without evidence to the contrary, it seems wise to assume the best. *Blue is not dead. Blue is free of Culver, whatever that might entail.* Fir could never have offered anything more than this.

"Are you leaving so you can look for Blue?" Fain asks.

"I'm not sure if I was really looking for Blue to begin with." Fir sighs.

"It might be okay if you weren't." Fain chances a glance at Fir, whose arid and vacant eyes are fastened to the dashboard, but Fain does not dare to lift a hand.

"I think that what I was really looking for was an answer. Closure. I just wanted a good reason to believe that Blue is alive and out there in the world somewhere. That Blue left, voluntarily." Fir explains. "And I have that now, I think. If I'm not invited into that life, well, I'll manage like I have for the past 20 years. No, not like I have. In some other way. The point is that I'll manage. I won't die languishing over Blue and whatever might have existed between us. Blue left; I can leave, too."

"Do you think," Fain hedges, "that Blue had anything to do with Culver's death?"

"No," Fir says emphatically. "That defies possibility."

"Do you think Blue is even aware that Culver is dead?"

"Maybe not, I guess. Maybe that's for the best. And if not, I won't be the one to bring that kind of guilt or grief or whatever else to Blue's door."

Fain looks away again, searching the field for another focal point and finding a jittery dragonfly, whose blue body glints as if it were moulded from a stolen piece of the sky, and who, alighting on the pod of a touch-me-not, sends forth a starburst of dark seeds.

NECROLUMINESCENCE

"I do not forgive you," Culver, standing in the foyer, said to an absent Blue. "I will not go looking for you." Culver insisted, walking through the door and locking up their house for the last time. "I will take nothing of you with me," Culver told the empty air of a grey early morning that was gauzy with mist, and threw the house keys into the flowerpot, where they disappeared beneath the cockled, soft-skinned petals of the blood-red gladioli.

Culver continued to recite these litanies to an absent Blue all through the long walk out of the suburbs, past the farms, beyond the trailer park. Each of these locales chafed with the friction of human need. People on the sidewalk wanted a greeting, or more of the path to themselves. Fences around tilled acres told passersby where the landowners expected them to go. The sign outside The Singing Frog trailer park requested a fee for entry onto the premises. Culver moved through these spaces, head down, eyes low, concentrating on the destination as the sun rose and sizzled away the last of the morning mist.

The mouth of the forest was dark, inviting to a certain kind of person, which Culver was. These woods had been deliberately chosen.

For their fatal power, of course, but also because they were the quietest place in Euphoria, insulated from interpersonal chaos, exempt, especially, from the handprints of Blue. It was land the two lovers had never seen together, though it was so close to the home they had shared for years.

Damp and warm and dark as it was, being in the Unwood felt like nestling in the organ of an enormous animal. Whatever understanding Culver had once shared with Blue now had to be, instead, transmogrified into an intimacy between Culver and this ecosystem that was both familiar and alien.

Culver took a small square of fabric from a pocket, then shed clothing, layer by layer, like a snake moulting, and buried the clothes beneath a small patch of loose soil. Sliding off glasses, and wedding band, Culver placed them too on top of the clothes. Then Culver reached for the class ring but found only bare skin on the middle finger of the right hand, and experienced a moment of panic, wondering when the class ring might have slipped off and whether it could be recovered, before realizing that it did not matter in the least what had become of it. Culver nearly laughed before swiftly turning solemn, unfolding the final small square of fabric. It was a sage green bonnet, infant-small, which Culver had embroidered with bluish harebells.

"You were never mine either, were you?" Culver said, seeming to address the hat, before covering the clothes, and glasses, and wedding band, and bonnet, over with dirt and the scree of dead foliage.

"I wanted it to be you, Blue," Culver murmured, descending into the arms of the thick grasses, reclining, pushing fingers into lush soil. Branches, heavy with the last of their summer leaves, blocked out the sky above almost completely.

"You can take me now," Culver said to the Unwood—

a polite and ritualistic formality, for Death would arrive, enormous and hungry, regardless of whether Culver called its name— and then lay still and waited.

First came the insects, nibbling at the epidermis, then the corium. Culver had expected it to hurt, but it didn't. It was easy, like when our hair falls out, or we lose our baby teeth. Overnight, the bacteria arrived, filling Culver's wounds with an oceanic glow. Aquamarine light spilled from the slits in Culver's dwindling form. On the second day, the deer ventured close, nosing at the motionless arms, licking the salt of sweat from Culver's forehead. Only once Culver had lapsed into the final, wakeless sleep of the afterlife did the coyote appear in the clearing, ready to finish the work.

SWEET

Fir and Fain have just sat down on Slip's couch when there is a knock at the trailer door. After flicking suspicious eyes in the direction of the guests, Slip goes cautiously to the door.

"Did you invite someone to tag along behind you?" Slip inquires before peering out.

"No, of course not," Fir returns.

"Well then who has the nerve to…oh." The door opens and in shuffle the kids.

"We saw you drive up," Mal tells Fir and Fain.

"Hello," Limn adds.

"I didn't realize we had a pop-over sort of relationship." The tone of Slip's statement is pitched somewhere between fond observation and complaint.

"Don't worry, we won't be expecting muffins," Mal replies lightly, settling uninvited and unabashed onto the kitchenette chair, while Limn idles tentatively in the doorway.

"Fine. Unless my company has any objections." Slip stares meaningfully at Fir and Fain. "Any at all."

"None," Fir answers. Is that a smirk? It disappears before Slip can decide.

"The kids are here because you're here and you're here why?" Slip asks Fir and Fain. "I don't think you mentioned yet."

"As I said before, I agree with you about not going to the police. And I think your decision to leave the bones in the woods makes sense as well, but we were thinking…" Fir turns, addresses Fain instead of Slip. "We were thinking it might be good to have some kind of, you know, memorial. A ceremony or something to acknowledge that someone died."

"Yes. It's important to acknowledge death explicitly," Slip says. "If we don't put up a tombstone, anyone passing by might mistake The Corpses for living people."

"I think it's a nice idea," Limn puts in.

"Do we really want to draw more attention to the bones than necessary?" Slip asks the room at large.

"If people go into that clearing, they're pretty likely to find the bones anyhow," Fir points out. "Besides, the sign can be small, inconspicuous. Even at a slight distance from the bones if you want."

"Is this important to you?" Slip presses. "Or do you just think it's the customary gesture you're supposed to make? Last I heard you didn't even like the person who died all that much."

"Oh, come on, Slip," Fain startles everyone by speaking for the first time. "You don't even really have a problem with the suggestion, do you?"

"Why do you say that?"

"You're obviously attached to the bones. You've *named* them."

Slip blushes, muttering, "I told you that in confidence."

"You've got a whole congregation," Fain waves a hand to indicate the four guests, "assembled around them. You're only disagreeing because you've lived alone so long that you've forgotten how to integrate other people's wishes into your own life."

"Thanks for the analysis," Slip grumbles. "Very incisive."

"I'm not wrong," Fain replies.

"I paint," Limn cuts in, and everyone turns to stare perplexed. "I can paint something. Like, on a rock maybe. So it'll last a pretty long time, several years probably, even though it's outside. And it's a rock so it can be painted again later if we want. And if we turn it face down it will just look like a rock. Nothing people will even notice. Unless they're walking around the Unwood turning over rocks, which seems unlikely."

"You're trying to weasel your way into seeing the bones, aren't you?" Slip asks.

"Yes," Mal answers.

"No," Limn says. "I'll just give you the rock once it's ready and you can take it to the bones."

It is possible, Slip realizes—over Mal's incredulous *What?*—that Limn's interest all along has not been morbid, as Slip long supposed, but the exact opposite. It might be more than possible, plausible even, that Limn has not been seeking to encounter the dead, but to confront the living.

"That sounds…" Eight eyes hover on Slip like honeybees investigating a flower. When did such a thing last happen, before today? Slip tries to recall. "Apt."

"We can get started on it today." Limn leaps up and tugs at Mal's sleeve. "We can do it right now."

CHANSON DE GESTE

"What kind of flower do you think it is?" Fain asks Slip and Fir, as the three of them regard the memorial rock Limn painted which sits, wordless, at the foot of a tree on the periphery of the Unwood, a short way off from where the bones repose. "A white daffodil maybe?"

"Hard to tell." Slip squints. "It could be a jonquil. Or a moonflower."

"An almond blossom," Fir suggests.

The three of them stand, facing the stone, childish and sincere in their clumsy approximation of funerary rites.

"Should we have added text to the stone?" Fain worries.

"Like what?" Fir asks.

"A word. Any word." Fain kneels, touches two fingers to the top of the stone.

"*Anonymous?*" Fir improvises. "*Anomaly? Anomie?*"

"Don't fuss." Slip says. "Kisses are a better fate than wisdom, and a flower is a better fate than some generic RIP."

"Should we at least offer a few words," Fain persists, "while we're all standing here?" Fain turns, expectant, toward Fir, who shrugs helplessly and turns toward Slip with pleading eyes.

"Well…" Having spoken so many times to the bones, Slip does not believe that anything more needs to be articulated. *Hello, goodbye,* these are phrases that Slip expects to repeat countless times to the bones when visiting them in the Unwood, and whatever peace or lack they have will be a condition of which Slip is also a part, so there is little need to wish for it.

A single, melancholy howl emerges from the woods. Other voices join, resounding high and several, surrounding the three people who stand astounded, casting glances all around them, in the clearing.

"Hello, song dogs," Slip says, as if a few humans had just arrived.

"Are those wolves?" Fir whispers.

"Coyotes," Slip answers, at regular volume.

"A whole pack of them?" Fir continues in a hushed tone. "Are we safe?"

"Could be two, could be ten. Not surprising this time of year. It's when all the young start to go off on their own, find new groups."

"Why is it so hard to say how many there are?"

"Any given coyote makes so many different and complicated sounds, it's hard for strangers like us to tell their voices apart. I think it's supposed to help them scare off predators and rivals, that kind of thing. Or maybe it's just a joke they like to play on unsuspecting visitors."

"I'm fine with leaving if they want us to leave."

"They'll let us alone if we don't approach them. They might not even be talking to us."

"You didn't spend much time outdoors as a child, did you?" Fain, who has been standing by silently, asks Fir.

"Not as an adult, either," Fir admits.

"I think it's sort of sweet," Fain says. "The coyotes are carrying the dirge."

"Just as well," Slip adds. "You wouldn't want to hear my warble."

"You could still add your melody to the chorus," Fain prompts.

"What would you have sung, Slip, if you had to?" Fir asks.

Slip sighs and then, hushed, so hushed it hardly sounds like words, but more like a susurrus of wind through brush, begins to hum, and then to sing.

Under the earth,
'neath grass and leaf
into the dark do our dead go.
But they return,
watered by grief,
in the faces of blooms that grow.

Slip coughs self-consciously. "I haven't thought of that tune for years. We sang it at the funeral of a family friend who died quite young. Drank too much. Liver gave out. I think they chose that song because it made the death seem like less of a hopeless waste."

MOURNING PORTRAITS

"I dunno, sounds kind of ghastly to me," Mal tells Limn. "I mean, obviously I support you and I'll help you with it, but that's just my honest opinion."

"Okay, it's ghastly," Limn admits. "So what?"

"People don't even want to look at *real* dead people."

"Yes, they do."

"Right, but they're not supposed to want to."

"Don't be so *modern*. Did you know that back when daguerreotypes became popular, they were still really expensive, so sometimes the only photographs people would have taken of them were after their deaths? Families took advantage of that last chance to have a likeness of their loved ones."

"You're on another research bender, I see."

The kids enter the trailer park and pass the management office, the landmark that, once attained, gives Limn the settled feeling of having arrived home.

"Anyways," Limn continues, "with what I'm doing, no one will even be looking at dead people. Really, they'll be looking at living people posed and painted to appear as if they were dead."

"Because that's so much better."

"It is. Death becomes familiar. Integrated into life. Then death will be less overwhelming when it actually arrives."

"I don't think my parents would agree."

"Well, I won't show them the painting of you then."

"Okay, whatever. If you want me to model so you can paint me up to look dead, I'll do it. But I still think it's abnormal."

"Yeah, probably. On the bright side, you don't have to strike a demanding pose or anything. You can basically just take a nap while I work."

"Sounds easy enough, I guess. Is this what you were thinking about while you were being a wallflower all night at the party?"

"I got the idea from someone I saw passed out on the couch."

"At least you actually came to a gathering of your peers for once."

"Hey," Limn points in the direction of Slip's trailer. "Look who's back."

They meander, magnetized but riverly, preferring not to seem too eager to reach their inevitable destination. As they approach, Limn is surprised to find two people playing backgammon on a folding table outside the trailer.

"Where's the other one?" Mal calls out, prompting Slip to look up from the game.

"Gone," Slip says.

"Taking some time away from Euphoria," Fain clarifies, still staring at the board.

Recognizing the deliberate evasiveness of euphemism, Limn puts on a look of wide-eyed naivete. "Why? Where?"

"Hard to say," Fain replies, disaffected.

"For how long?"

"Until the day Fir returns," Slip says with tautological finality.

Limn turns, whispers into the shell of the Mal's ear.

"Maybe I should ask them."

"Don't."

"Why not? I think I'm owed a favour."

Mal leans back, considers, leans in again.

"Actually, you're right. These are probably two of the only people we know who might hear about your project and still be willing to talk to you afterwards."

"Yes, exactly, thank you."

"What are you two scheming about?" Slip asks.

Gingerly balancing dismissiveness and indulgence, Mal handles the question: "*Someone,*" here Mal points a thumb at Limn, "thinks it would be a fun casual project to paint living people as if they were dead and is looking for volunteer models."

"Oh, I am so out," Fain says immediately.

"Hmm." Slip deliberates. "I will probably never get a chance to see myself when I'm dead. It could be interesting to see it now."

"Really?" Limn asks.

"Sure," Slip says. "But you have to really set a scene. Let me out, roadside, wearing leather and aviators, clutching a pineapple."

"Why a pineapple?"

Slip shrugs. "Why roadside? It adds narrative potential. Gives people something to think about."

"I'm sure you two can negotiate something," Mal says.

"Thanks," Limn adds.

"But for now, we'll leave you to your game." Mal finishes and the kids step away. Limn offers a tentative wave, which Fain returns with equal hesitancy.

"Yes, and you two should try to go to bed before noon," Slip says, with an inflection that might be mistaken for care.

ECHIUM VULGARE

Weed to some, wildflower to others, the lush corolla of *Echium Vulgare* can transmute from dusky pink to afterglow blue on even the most impoverished land, like this glassy sand of a freshwater shoreline a few miles north of Lac Lemot. Possessed of nutlets formed like viperous heads, it has been said that *Echium Vulgare*, which also goes by the name Blueweed, can nullify the bite of a real reptilian snake, though whether that rumour is true no one can now recall. It scarcely matters here, for snakes have little interest in the beach of a cold lake. This *Echium Vulgare* rises precariously skyward, vulnerable to gravity and aggressive vines, though both of these it meets with a gritty if finite persistence, snarling its roots further and more securely into the earth, coiling through bloodied satin and black strands of human hair.

FUNGICULTURE

A small crowd of students is assembled in the dim shed, their faces vegetal and faintly green in the viridian light radiating from a cluster of bitter oyster mushrooms.

"They are particularly bright right now," the instructor explains, "because they are undergoing spore maturation. This species is significant not only as an example of bioluminscence, but also because of its potential applications in bioremediation. It has been shown to reduce the presence of toxic levels of polyphenols in wastewater. High concentrations of polyphenols result from various industrial processes such as fabric dyeing and olive debittering. This species may also help clean land contaminated by other kinds of organic pollutants. Research is ongoing in this area." A switch is flicked and a faint bulb sputters to life overhead, making visible the panoply of mushroom species growing in the shed.

The jelly-soft wood ears, for instance, which emanate from the bark of the dead tree at the front of the class, make it appear as if the tree is listening to the group of visitors assembled before it. Though the wood ears are many, they actually constitute a single organism, held together by impossibly gauzy wisps of mycelium. The instructor is still speaking—rhapsodizing now about honey fungi that are thousands of years old, thousands of tonnes heavy, thousands of acres wide, too vast to measure except by the vaguest of estimates— but Fir, feet numb and legs restless with cold, soundlessly tiptoes out the door of the shed.

Outside, the sunlit October air is scarcely warmer, but it is far drier and brighter than the dim and dewy cloud in which the fungi grow. Every week, Fir leaves class early, but the next week still returns, bewitched by the mushrooms, those fleshy psychopomps who intercede between the living and the dead, turning one into the other and the other into the one.

The mushroom shed is a modest A-frame structure in the small but flourishing community garden that is mere blocks beyond downtown Valence. Today, as has become customary after class, Fir sets out on the 15-minute walk that leads to a barely-populated café off the main street, where Fir has made a ritual of proceeding alphabetically, visit by visit, through the long list of loose-leaf teas. Some familiar, like chamomile, others unexpected, like fennel, none of them as exhilarating as coffee, which is just as well, for often Fir finds that the central nervous system more than justifies its name, amply frenetic even when confronting ordinary life.

Transparent as a fishbowl, the whole front of the café is windows, including the door, which today slips, suddenly slick, through Fir's hand before it can even be opened. Reflected in the glass, Fir sees, across the street, a familiar figure walking. Fir turns around to get a direct look. Collar up, head down, but how could it be anyone else?

Fir is sure; Fir is not sure; Fir is sure enough.

Here, on the shore of the sidewalk, Fir stands fast. There, on the far shore, Blue walks away. And between them, a lake, throwing breathless fish at their feet.

ACKNOWLEDGMENTS

I don't know how I ever finished writing a novel, but I do know I was helped along the way.

To my thesis committee: Drs. Louis Cabri, Carol Margaret Davison, and the late great Catherine Hundleby (1966-2023). Thank you, Dr. Cabri, for your grounding calm and artistic curiosity during our weekly mid-pandemic telephone meetings. Dr. Davison, you were an inspiring and encouraging mentor when I was a student in your wonderful classes on Gothic literature. Thank you for prodding my novel along while you were writing your own. And thank you Dr. Hundleby. Wherever you are now, I'm sure you're casting your astute philosophical eye upon your surroundings.

Thank you to the University of Windsor and the Ontario Graduate Scholarship program for giving me two years to work.

Thank you to other early readers of this project: long-time editor and annotator of my writing, Jeremy Colangelo, whose own novel I eagerly await; Hafizah Geter, who owed me nothing but generously gave me great advice anyway—if there's powder in this novel it's because of you; Caitlin Galway, who is a freelance editor I cannot recommend highly enough, and whose forthcoming short fiction collection I am so looking forward to reading.

Utmost thanks to Corinna Chong, Michael Melgaard, and Aaron Tucker for their deeply insightful words about *Anomia*, which describe the book better than I ever could.

Thank you to my fellow poet-at-heart Kamila Rina, an excellent friend with whom to walk this genderweird road.

Thank you Ari for all the days you spent sitting on my desk beside the hibiscuses while I wrote. I'll miss you forever. Thank you Lulu for doing your best to take over Ari's shift after he had to pack his metaphysical suitcase and go.

Thank you to the Palimpsest Press team for their crucial efforts to bring this odd little project into the world. Aimée Parent Dunn, I dearly appreciate you letting me be a tad precious about my first novel. Vanessa Shields, I'm grateful for your cheerful, enthusiastic championing of the press' titles.

Thank you, as always, to my parents, Laurie and James Wallace, for filling our house with books and philosophical debate.

Extra thanks to my mother, for being the single absolutely loyal fan of my writing throughout the years.

Finally, thank you to Mark Laliberte, my eleventh hour editor, and my other half both on the page and in the home. As you already know, I'm grateful for your gorgeous design work on this book, and all of my books, and all of our books. I'm glad we've chosen to permanently combine our libraries.

First Edition.
June, 2024

PALIMPSEST PRESS
1171 Eastlawn Ave
Windsor, ON
N8S 3J1

info@palimpsestpress.ca

palimpsestpress.ca

Jade Wallace (they/them) is a queer writer, editor, and critic, as well as co-founder of the collaborative writing entity MA|DE. Wallace is the author of two poetry collections, *Love Is A Place But You Cannot Live There* (2023) and *The Work Is Done When We Are Dead* (2026), both with Guernica Editions. MA|DE's debut poetry collection, *ZZOO* (2025), is forthcoming from Palimpsest Press.

JADEWALLACE.CA

MA-DE.CA